Praise for *The Dangerous Book for Boys*

'The perfect handbook for boys and dads.'

*Daily Telegraph*

'Full of tips on how to annoy your parents.'

*Evening Standard*

'An old-fashioned compendium of information on items such as making catapults and knot-tying... the end of the PlayStation may have been signalled.'

*The Times*

'Just William would be proud. A new book teaching boys old-fashioned risky pursuits has become a surprise bestseller.'

*Daily Mail*

'If you want to know how to make crystals, master NATO's phonetic alphabet and build a workbench, look no further.'

*Time Out*

# THE POCKET DANGEROUS BOOK FOR BOYS:

# FACTS, FIGURES AND FUN

A collection of fascinating facts that every boy should know selected from *The Dangerous Book for Boys* and *The Dangerous Book for Boys Yearbook.*

This edition is a perfect pocket format for readers to take everywhere with them.

Visit www.dangerousbook.co.uk for quizzes, games and more.

**Also by Conn and Hal Iggulden:**

*The Dangerous Book for Boys*
*The Dangerous Book for Boys Yearbook*
*The Pocket Dangerous Book for Boys: Things to Do*
*The Pocket Dangerous Book for Boys: Things to Know*
*The Pocket Dangerous Book for Boys: Wonders of the World*

**Also by Conn Iggulden:**

The Emperor series
*The Gates of Rome*
*The Death of Kings*
*The Field of Swords*
*The Gods of War*

The Conqueror series
*Wolf of the Plains*
*Lords of the Bow*
*Bones of the Hills*

*Blackwater*

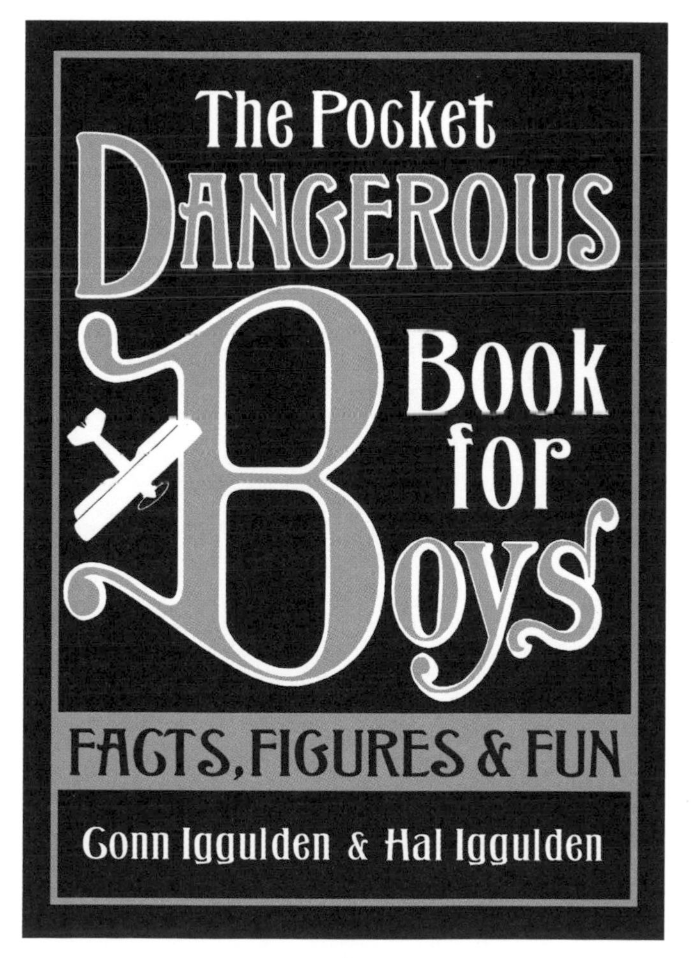

HarperCollins*Publishers*

HarperCollins*Publishers*
77–85 Fulham Palace Road,
Hammersmith, London W6 8JB

www.harpercollins.co.uk

Published by HarperCollins*Publishers* 2008
1

A catalogue record for this book
is available from the British Library

ISBN-13: 978 0 00 728472 6

Set in Centennial CE 55 Roman by Envy Design Ltd

Printed and bound in Italy by
L.E.G.O. SpA - Vicenza

To all of those people who said 'You *have* to include ...' until we had to avoid telling anyone else about the book for fear of the extra chapters. Particular thanks to Bernard Cornwell, whose advice helped us through a difficult time and Paul D'Urso, a good father and a good friend.

# CONTENTS

# INTRODUCTION

I THINK I KNOW WHY boys in particular like strange and interesting facts. From my own time before regular shaving, I remember thinking it gave me some control over the world, that I could *own* it in some small way by knowing Charles II hid in an oak tree, or that arsenic poisoning makes your hair fall out. As a boy, I sometimes delivered ominous warnings that balding relatives should check their food.

The fact that painting the Forth bridge never stops – they reach the end and then begin again immediately – is one of those things that every schoolboy used to know. It's tempting to dismiss this kind of knowledge as the same sort of geekiness that can name all the characters in *Star Trek*, or explain how to create a Paladin in Dungeons and Dragons. However, in the same way that stories create culture, facts do as well. If we all know that bad King John lost the crown jewels, or even that a falling man accelerates at 22ft per second/per second until he reaches a terminal velocity, it creates a shared bank of knowledge. In this day and age, of course, there's nothing wrong with knowing the population of China, or the trade surplus of Canada, but this book is more often concerned with those peculiarly British bits of knowledge. I really like knowing that an MP cannot be described as drunk in parliament, but instead is 'tired and emotional'. I love knowing that if an MP dies in the House of Commons, he or she has to be carried outside to avoid the need to give them a State funeral they almost certainly don't deserve.

Knowledge changes, of course. More long-lasting paint means the Forth bridge is now *not* painted continuously. It is also no longer true that 'Habeas Corpus' – literally, 'I have the body' – prevents innocent men and women from being locked up without trial in Britain. They can now be locked up for forty-two days, then set free without even an apology. That's a slightly embarrassing one to explain to my children, but not all facts are easy to swallow. Perhaps that example shows the need to understand the society around us – and the importance of hard won liberties that were taken for granted just a generation ago.

I like the fact that Edmund Hillary never said who stepped onto the peak of Everest first – he or Tensing Norgay. It makes me proud, that. The knowledge of childhood should be as wide-ranging as possible. Especially today, it is our only chance to enjoy *everything* before we have to begin funnelling our knowledge into A-levels, degrees or a career. My older brother once said he wished they'd mentioned in school that trigonometry is about finding your position at sea. Teachers always mention the less than exciting example of discovering the height of a tall building. Personally, I'd climb it and drop a string down, then measure the string ... But at sea, with a sextant, you really need to know your triangles.

Why bother though, in a world of GPS and satellites? It isn't enough to say they sometimes break. There is a sense of enormous personal satisfaction in being able to do something for *yourself*, from crossing a road for the first time to building a shed, or calculating your latitude from the height of the sun at noon.

It doesn't need to be useful, that's the thing. Knowing the highest mountain on earth is actually Hawaii, if you measure from the bottom to the top, is never going to impress friends and influence people, but I still like having it on one of the shelves in my brain.

It has been said that the more you learn, the less you realise you know and that is probably true, but that's no reason to stop, it really isn't.

Conn Iggulden

# GREAT MEN

George Washington was elected as the first President of the United States in February 1789.

❖

The Apache leader Geronimo died at the age of 80. Geronimo was actually a nickname given to him by Mexican soldiers. His real name was Goyaalé, sometimes spelled Goyathlay. It means 'yawner'. He led the last major force of Native American Indians in resistance against the white settlers, finally surrendering in 1886. His daring exploits meant that the name Geronimo became synonymous with wild bravery. It is still shouted today by parachutists and anyone else attempting something dangerous.

❖

In 1815 Napoleon escaped from the Island of Elba, beginning the Hundred Days' War, which ended at Waterloo. He died on the island of St Helena in 1821.

Charles Darwin, born in 1809, was one of the great minds of the nineteenth century. At the age of only 20, he took part in a scientific expedition on HMS *Beagle* to South America and, most famously, the Galapagos islands, off the coast of Ecuador. There, Darwin found giant tortoises and iguanas that evolved differently in the isolated islands. He also found species of birds unique to the islands. After returning to England, he went on to write *The Origin of Species* and formulate the theory of evolution. He was also one of the last scientific non-specialists: a naturalist, biologist, geologist, author, illustrator, taxidermist and medical student.

❖

Horatio Nelson was born at Burnham Thorpe in Norfolk on 29 September 1758. He went on to become quite a successful Royal Navy Admiral. With Wellington, he clobbered Napoleon.

Michelangelo di Lodovico Buonarroti Simoni was born in Tuscany. He went on to produce the greatest sculptures and paintings in history. His most famous work is perhaps La Pietà, a s̀culpture of Mary holding the body of Jesus across her knees. He is also famed as the painter of the Sistine Chapel in Rome, for his statue David and numerous other works. He was

a Renaissance man in the literal sense of living in the Renaissance period, but Michelangelo was one of those who led to the term meaning 'skilled in many arts'. An architect, sculptor and painter, he lived at the same time as Leonardo da Vinci. The two men disliked each other intensely, which is perhaps not surprising.

Admiral Lord Collingwood, born in Newcastle, was a great friend of Nelson's and their tombs lie in the same section of the Undercroft in St Paul's Cathedral. It was Collingwood who fired the first shot at Trafalgar in 1805, prompting Nelson to say, 'See how that noble fellow Collingwood carries his ship into action!' Collingwood took command on Nelson's death. He met Nelson first in Jamaica, when they were both midshipmen. They were friends ever after.

❖

The theoretical physicist and mathematician Albert Einstein is best known for his theory of relativity and his influence on the Manhattan Project, which led to the first atomic bomb. Einstein was a Nobel Prize winner and his name has become synonymous with genius. He had an unusually large head. His last words are unknown as he spoke in German and the nurse did not understand that language.

Julius Caesar was born *c.* 100 BC, in the fifth month of the Roman calendar known as *Quintilis*. The name of the month was later changed to July in his honour. He famously crossed the Rubicon and began a civil war.

Lord Louis Mountbatten became the last Viceroy of India in 1947, helping to negotiate the independence of Pakistan and India from British rule. Mahatma Gandhi called the process 'the noblest act of the British Nation'. Mountbatten, a hero of World War II, was later killed by an IRA bomb in 1979.

### Oddities

In 1953 the 'Piltdown man' skull was revealed as a hoax. At first the skull was believed to be the 'missing link' in evolution, proving a connection between mankind and apes, as had been theorized. 'Discovered' in 1911, the skull was put together using the jawbone of an orangutan. The best suspect for the identity of the hoaxer is Charles Dawson, who found the skull. However, no one ever admitted to it.

GREAT MEN

8

Genghis Khan conquered an area four times larger than that gained by Alexander the Great. His ruthlessness is legendary, though much of that image comes from history written by those he conquered. He died at the age of 55 after falling from a horse, though the date is not absolutely certain. Legends persist that he was stabbed by a woman and eventually lost too much blood to stay in the saddle. In Mongolia he is considered the heroic father of the nation. His sons went on to enlarge his empire, and his grandson, Kublai, became emperor of a united China.

❖

John Stuart Mill, one of the great thinkers of the nineteenth century, was born on 20 May 1806. His essays and books, particularly *On Liberty*, are vital reading even today.

❖

Alexander the Great died in 232 BC, after a fever. He was only 33. He never lost a battle.

The feast day of the Venerable Bede is on 25 May. He is known as the 'Father of English History' for his work *The Ecclesiastical History of the English Nation*, written in the early eighth century. He was the first writer in English prose and is the only Englishman mentioned by Dante in his *Paradiso*.

In AD 899, Alfred the Great died. He was buried in Newminster Abbey, Winchester. The only king to have the title 'Great', Alfred beat the Danes, helped to unify England and began the navy.

**ODDITIES**

Winston Churchill permanently abolished ID cards in 1952.

# OZYMANDIAS

I met a traveller from an antique land
Who said: Two vast and trunkless legs of stone
Stand in the desert. Near them on the sand,
Half sunk, a shatter'd visage lies, whose frown
And wrinkled lip and sneer of cold command
Tell that its sculptor well those passions read
Which yet survive, stamp'd on these lifeless things,
The hand that mock'd them and the heart that fed.
And on the pedestal these words appear:
'My name is Ozymandias, king of kings:
Look on my works, ye Mighty, and despair!'
Nothing beside remains: round the decay
Of that colossal wreck, boundless and bare,
The lone and level sands stretch far away.

PERCY BYSSHE SHELLEY, 1792–1822

# POOR DEALS

In 1695, a window tax was introduced in Britain. It seemed obvious that the more windows a house had, the wealthier the owners had to be. An unforeseen side-effect of this tax was that many windows on large houses were bricked up by their irate owners.

❖

Native Americans sold Manhattan to the Dutch Trading Company who established a fort in what they called New Amsterdam in 1626 for 60 guilders, or about $1 per thousand acres. In 1664 the English conquered it, renaming it New York. At the end of the war, the Dutch let the English keep it in exchange for Run, a small island in the East Indies, then perceived as more valuable.

### Odd Days

The ancient pagan feast day of Beltane, which celebrates spring, is on 1 May. In ancient Rome it was the Festival of Fools, where society's rules could be broken without punishment. In Britain it is also known as Gosling Day, or Horse Ribbon Day.

In 1803 France turned New Orleans over to the United States as part of the Louisiana Purchase, where America bought a fifth of their entire country from French ownership for $27¼ million, roughly 3 cents an acre. It is worth pointing out that the reason the French were willing to sell the land is because Napoleon was fighting Britain and desperately needed money.

❖

In 1887 Russia sold Alaska to the USA for $7 million. They saw it as a frozen, worthless wilderness. Later, oil was found.

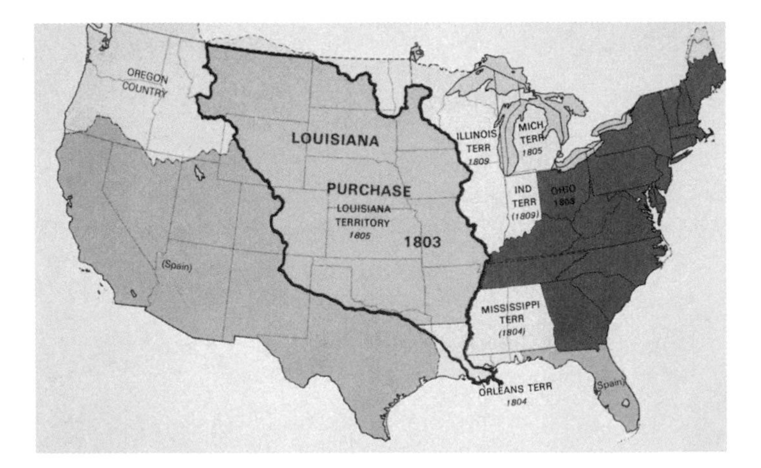

### Oddities

Before 'decimalization' in 1971, British coin values were based around the number 12 rather than 10. There were 12 pennies to a shilling and 20 shillings to a pound – so 240 pennies in a pound. A guinea was a pound and a shilling – so 21 shillings. Guineas survive today in certain high-price areas such as the sale of racehorses. In those auctions, it is possible to bid in pounds and have someone shout 'Guineas' to top the bid.

Shillings and pennies were originally silver coins. Shillings were introduced in 1504 and pennies much earlier, perhaps back in the fifth century at the time that the Romans withdrew from Britain. In 'old' money (before 1971), pennies were written with the symbol 'd' which stood for denarius – a Roman silver coin.

The reason British money is called a pound is because 240 silver pennies weighed 12 ounces – the exact weight of a Roman pound. It is also interesting to know that the '£' symbol is a short form for the imperial weight measurement of a pound 'lb', which stands for the Latin word for pound, libra.

INVENTORS

John Boyd Dunlop was the inventor of the pneumatic rubber tyre – and also the word 'pneumatic'. The Dunlop company still makes car tyres today.

Frank Whittle invented the jet engine. He lived until 1996, seeing his invention used all over the world. He is commemorated in the RAF chapel in Westminster Abbey.

In 1876 Alexander Graham Bell sent the world's first telephone message to his assistant Thomas Watson. The spectacularly uninspiring words were: 'Mr Watson, come here. I want you.' In 1878, Bell demonstrated his invention to Queen Victoria. She was on it for hours.

❖

John Logie Baird, a Scottish inventor, gave the world's first demonstration of television in 1926, in his attic, to around fifty scientists. He would later achieve the first transatlantic transmission, the first live transmission in 1931 and the first demonstration of colour television.

❖

Charles Babbage, who was born in Teignmouth in 1791, went on to invent the calculating machine that was the forerunner of computers.

The world's first recording of a human voice was heard in 1877. The inventor of the 'Phonograph', Thomas Edison, recorded himself reciting 'Mary had a little lamb' and played it back.

## Odd Days

February is the shortest month, with 28 days, or 29 in leap years. A leap year is when the number of the year is exactly divisible by four. Dates exactly divisible by 100 are exceptions. They are not leap years unless they are also divisible by 400, like the year 2000. It's a bit complicated, but there's nothing wrong with that.

Traditionally, women are allowed to propose to men on 29 February. The origin of the custom is unknown, though there is an apocryphal story about a conversation between St Bridget and St Patrick, where she complained that women could not ask men to marry them. He suggested that they could do so every seven years and she bargained him down to four. It is also traditional that if a woman is refused on this day, the man must buy her a silk gown.

Sir Hiram Maxim was a US-born British inventor. His most famous invention, named after him, was the first fully automatic machine gun, used by both sides in World War I. He also invented the 'Captive Flying Machine' fairground ride, with small carriages attached to poles that whip round and give the illusion of flying. There is still one 1904 original in operation at Blackpool Pleasure Beach.

James Dyson invented the Dual Cyclone bagless vacuum cleaner. It took 4,500 prototypes to arrive at one good enough to sell. For that level of determination alone, he deserves his place here.

**To Remember the Colours of the Rainbow**

*Richard of York Gave Battle In Vain.*

Red, orange, yellow, green, blue, indigo, violet.

The Swiss Officer's knife was patented in 1887. It became a staple of all camping trips and the like, though most people who use one have a story of the blade closing on their fingers and gashing them deeply. The Leatherman multi-tool, with its locking blades and decent-sized pliers, is much better for all-round use, though it does lack a corkscrew.

## The Burial of John Moore after Corunna

Not a drum was heard, not a funeral note,
As his corse to the rampart we hurried;
Not a soldier discharged his farewell shot
O'er the grave where our hero we buried.

We buried him darkly at dead of night,
The sods with our bayonets turning,
By the struggling moonbeam's misty light
And the lanthorn dimly burning.

No useless coffin enclosed his breast,
Not in sheet or in shroud we wound him;
But he lay like a warrior taking his rest
With his martial cloak around him.

Few and short were the prayers we said,
And we spoke not a word of sorrow;
But we steadfastly gazed on the face that was dead,
And we bitterly thought of the morrow.

We thought, as we hollow'd his narrow bed
And smooth'd down his lonely pillow,
That the foe and the stranger would tread o'er his head,
And we far away on the billow!

Lightly they'll talk of the spirit that's gone,
And o'er his cold ashes upbraid him –
But little he'll reck, if they let him sleep on
In the grave where a Briton has laid him.

But half of our heavy task was done
When the clock struck the hour for retiring;
And we heard the distant and random gun
That the foe was sullenly firing.

Slowly and sadly we laid him down,
From the field of his fame fresh and gory;
We carved not a line, and we raised not a stone,
But we left him alone with his glory.

CHARLES WOLFE, 1791–1823

SPORTING DRAMA
AAA
41

In 1954 Roger Bannister broke the four-minute mile for the first time.

❖

John L. Sullivan defeated Jake Kilrain after a 75-round bare-knuckle heavyweight boxing match in 1889. Sullivan vomited in the forty-fourth round, but recovered to win. He was the last bare-knuckle champion. Later champions have fought under the rules devised by the Marquis of Queensbury, with gloves.

❖

In 1896 the first modern Olympic games was held in Athens. A Greek, Spyridon Louis, won the marathon. An Irishman, John Boland, was on holiday in Greece at the time and entered the men's tennis competition. To his surprise, he won the gold medal.

**STILL A USEFUL WEATHER FORECAST**

*Red sky in the morning, shepherd's warning,*
*Red sky at night, shepherd's delight.*

The boxer Joe Louis became heavyweight world champion in 1937, knocking out Jim Braddock. He had only ever been beaten by one man in his career – Max Schmeling, cast by Nazi propaganda as an ideal Aryan warrior. Joe Louis said he would not consider himself champion until he had fought Schmeling again. A year after winning the title, he did. When Schmeling went down in the first round, Goebbels ordered the radio transmission to Germany to be cut off. Joe Louis won a convincing victory, though Germany didn't hear it. Louis held the title for eleven years, eight months and nine days, the longest heavyweight reign to date.

The American swimmer Johnny Weissmuller was the first person to swim 100 metres in less than a minute. He went on to set more than sixty swimming world records and win five Olympic golds. He is, however, more famous for playing Tarzan in twelve films, beginning with *Tarzan the Ape Man*. He is often seen swimming and wrestling with alligators. His ululating Tarzan yell was so good that it was used in later films with other actors.

Yours Truly
Joe Louis

England won the World Cup in 1966, beating Germany 4–2 at Wembley Stadium. It was 2–2 at the end of normal time, then in extra time Geoff Hurst scored a controversial goal, causing much debate as to whether it crossed the goal line or not. It did, though, so that's enough of that. Hurst scored again in the final minute. The BBC commentator, Kenneth Wolstenholme, said famously, 'Some people are on the pitch. They think it's all over ... it is now! It's four!'

Andy Green, who set the world land speed record in the car Thrust SSC in 1997, drove the world's fastest diesel – the JCB Dieselmax – at the Bonneville salt flats in America in 2006, reaching a speed of 328 mph.

## Vitaï Lampada

There's a breathless hush in the Close tonight –
  Ten to make and the match to win -
A bumping pitch and a blinding light,
  An hour to play and the last man in.
And it's not for the sake of the ribboned coat,
  Or the selfish hope of a season's fame,
But his Captain's hand on his shoulder smote –
  'Play up! play up! and play the game!'

The sand of the Desert is sodden red –
  Red with the wreck of a square that broke; –
The Gatling's jammed and the Colonel's dead,
  And the regiment's blind with dust and smoke.
The river of death has brimmed his banks,
  And England's far, and Honour a name,
But the voice of a schoolboy rallies the ranks:
  'Play up! play up! and play the game!'

This is the world that year by year,
While in her place the school is set,
Every one of her sons must hear,
And none that hears it dare forget.
This they all with joyful mind
Bear through life like a torch in flame,
And falling fling to the host behind –
'Play up! play up! and play the game!'

SIR HENRY NEWBOLT, 1862–1938

# GRUESOME DEATHS

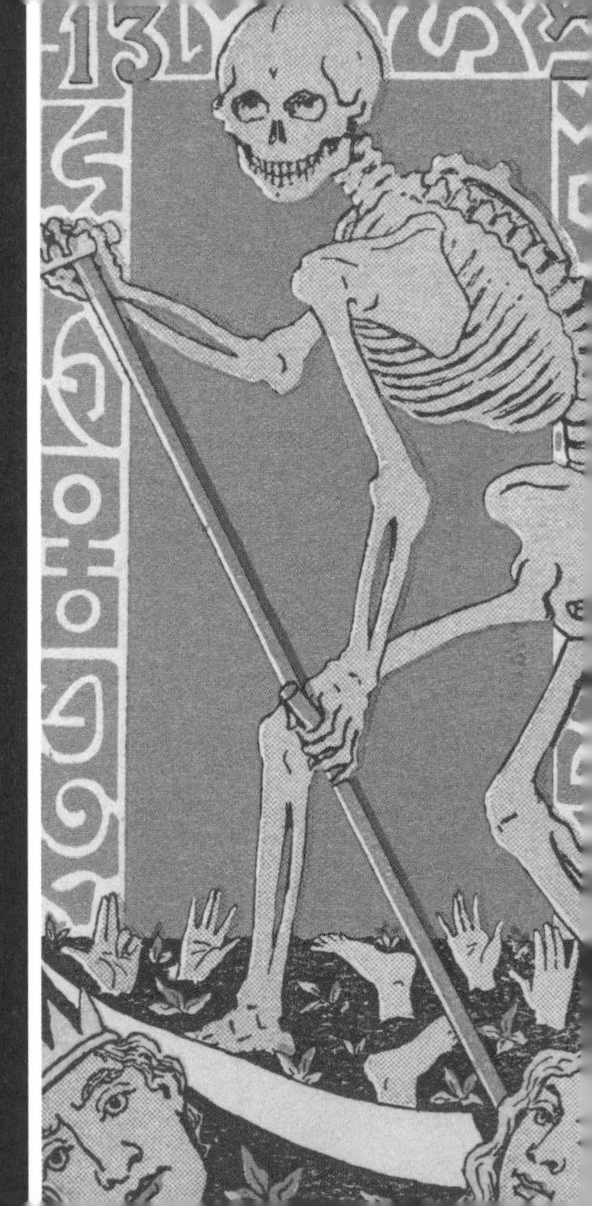

The Nazi propagandist William Joyce was hanged for treason in January 1946. Most famous for broadcasts to Britain during World War II that began 'Germany calling, Germany calling ...', Joyce is better known as 'Lord Haw-Haw'.

❖

The execution of Anne Boleyn, Henry VIII's second wife and mother to Elizabeth I, took place on 19 May 1536. She stood accused of adultery with several men, including her husband's tennis coach and her own brother George, which doesn't seem very likely. A French executioner was brought from Calais. A swordsman, it was thought that he might do a cleaner job than an axe-man, who sometimes took two or three blows to remove a head. When Anne heard this, she said, 'He shall not have much trouble, for I have a little neck.' When the time came, it took a single blow, and she was buried in a chapel at the Tower of London.

Mary Ann Nichols, the first victim of Jack the Ripper, was found mutilated in Whitechapel, London, in 1888. At least five other victims followed and the particularly grisly murders became famous throughout the world. Despite a number of theories as to his identity, the murderer was never caught.

James Butler Hickok, better known as Wild Bill Hickok, was shot dead at a saloon in the town of Deadwood in 1876. He never usually played poker with his back to the door, but on that day there was no other seat. As Hickok picked up his cards, a man named Jack McCall entered and shot him in the back of the head. The motive for the murder is uncertain, though it may have been rage born of humiliation. Hickok had offered to buy McCall breakfast after he had lost his money the previous day. The hand Hickok held was pairs of aces and eights, with the fifth card unknown. It is still called the Dead Man's Hand. Before his death, he was a legendary sheriff and gunfighter of the old West.

The Catholic conspirator Guy Fawkes was executed – hanged, drawn and quartered – on 31 January 1606. He was one of the members of the Gunpowder Plot, an attempt to blow up the Houses of Parliament and assassinate King James I. The discovery of this consipiracy is still celebrated every year on 5 November.

❖

In 1945 the Norwegian traitor Vidkun Quisling was executed. Quisling had collaborated openly with the Nazis. The word 'Quisling' is still used to mean traitor.

❖

The execution of King Charles I by Cromwell took place in 1649 in Whitehall. Charles I wore two shirts as it was a cold morning and he didn't want the crowd to see him shiver and think he was afraid. He was allowed to walk his dog in St James's Park before the execution. When he was dead, the crowd paid to dip handkerchiefs in his royal blood.

The Gunfight at the OK Corral took place in Tombstone, Arizona, on 26 October 1881. It is perhaps the most famous gunfight in the history of the Wild West. Marshal Virgil Earp, his brothers Wyatt and Morgan and Doc Holliday, shot it out with Frank McLaury, Tom McLaury, Ike Clanton, Billy Clanton and Billy Claibourne. Around thirty shots were fired in as many seconds. Both the McLaurys and Billy Clanton were killed. Virgil and Morgan Earp were later shot in revenge, though Virgil survived without the use of his right arm. Wyatt Earp came through unscathed.

The highwayman Dick Turpin was hanged in York in 1739.

### Odd Days

21 April 753 BC is the traditional date for the founding of Rome by twin brothers named Romulus and Remus. Romulus would later murder Remus.

In 1916 the 'mad monk' Grigory Rasputin was killed, a surprisingly difficult thing to accomplish. He had become a guru to the Russian tsar and his family and was considered by some to be a malign influence on them. A group of nobles poisoned Rasputin's wine and food, but he thrived on it. When that failed, they shot him and he collapsed. To their astonishment, he came round quickly, leaped up and half-strangled one of his assailants before trying to flee the palace grounds. He was shot three more times in the process, which didn't stop him. The final attempt involved tying him up and throwing him into a freezing river. His body was later recovered and the official cause of death given as drowning.

Thomas à Becket, the Archbishop of Canterbury, was killed by four knights at an altar in Canterbury Cathedral, later to become a place of pilgrimage until Henry VIII had the remains burnt. King Henry II, having been denied revenues by Thomas, shouted, 'Who will rid me of this turbulent priest?' and the four knights set out, believing they were doing his bidding. After the murder, Henry II submitted to being whipped in public as penance for his part in the deed.

Lord Chancellor Sir Thomas More was executed for treason in London in 1535, having refused to accept Henry VIII as head of the Church of England. He was canonized in 1935 on the 400th anniversary of his martyrdom. Robert Bolt's play *A Man for All Seasons* is a superb examination of the characters and arguments involved.

The tragic Lady Jane Grey was the granddaughter of Henry VIII's sister. An attempt to take the crown on her behalf was arranged by the Duke of Northumberland. Lady Jane Grey was married to his son, Lord Dudley. Although she was declared the official heir by a dying Edward VI, neither Lords nor Commons would accept her over Mary I, Henry VIII's oldest daughter. Lady Jane reigned for only nine days. She and her husband were both beheaded on 12 February 1554.

In 1882 the outlaw Jesse James was shot dead at the age of 35 by a member of his own gang.

Mary Queen of Scots, Catholic cousin to England's Elizabeth I, had a tragic life. After a failed rebellion against Elizabeth, she was imprisoned for eighteen years and eventually tried on charges of treason. At her trial, she said: 'Remember, gentlemen, the Theatre of History is wider than the Realm of England.' Unlike the clean stroke that beheaded Anne Boleyn, it took three blows to remove Mary's head. When Elizabeth I died without heirs, Mary's son united the thrones as James I of England and VI of Scotland.

❖

The infamous Dr Crippen was arrested at sea for the murder of his wife. He was the first criminal to be caught by the use of radio and was later hanged at Pentonville Prison.

❖

William Wallace, the Scottish war leader, had an incredibly brutal death. He was first part-hanged, then 'drawn', which means ripped open while still alive. He was then castrated, eviscerated, beheaded and his body cut into four pieces. His head was placed on a pike in London, joined by that of his brother John.

Captain Cook and his crew were welcomed as gods in Hawaii, until one of them died, giving the game away. The native islanders took a dim view of the deception and killed him. One of the men who collected Cook's dismembered body parts was William Bligh, most famous for the later mutiny on the *Bounty*.

Sir Nicholas Carew, once a favourite of King Henry VIII and a very accomplished knight, was beheaded for treason. He was present at 'The Field of the Cloth of Gold', Henry VIII's meeting near Calais with the French king. At the jousting on that day, Carew was successful against all-comers and not unhorsed. He was a distant relative of Anne Boleyn and also jousted successfully at her coronation. The story goes that when Henry VIII spoke rudely to him at a game of bowls, Carew forgot caution and replied in the same manner, deeply offending the king. Eventually, he was charged with exchanging letters with Exeter, a traitor. Carew was executed at Tower Hill, London.

Mussolini was executed by Italian resistance fighters in 1945. He was shot repeatedly. His body was publicly displayed and then shot again, just to make absolutely certain.

In 1701 Captain William Kidd was hanged for piracy and murder in London, having made the mistake of preying on English vessels. He was originally employed by the crown to hunt pirates, but went to the bad himself in 1697.

## Dulce et Decorum Est

Bent double, like old beggars under sacks,
Knock-kneed, coughing like hags, we cursed through sludge,
Till on the haunting flares we turned our backs
And towards our distant rest began to trudge.
Men marched asleep. Many had lost their boots
But limped on, blood-shod. All went lame; all blind;
Drunk with fatigue; deaf even to the hoots
Of tired, outstripped Five-Nines that dropped behind.
Gas! Gas! Quick, boys! – An ecstasy of fumbling,
Fitting the clumsy helmets just in time;
But someone still was yelling out and stumbling,
And flound'ring like a man in fire or lime . . .
Dim, through the misty panes and thick green light,
As under a green sea, I saw him drowning.
In all my dreams, before my helpless sight,
He plunges at me, guttering, choking, drowning.
If in some smothering dreams you too could pace
Behind the wagon that we flung him in,

And watch the white eyes writhing in his face,
His hanging face, like a devil's sick of sin;
If you could hear, at every jolt, the blood
Come gargling from the froth-corrupted lungs,
Obscene as cancer, bitter as the cud
Of vile, incurable sores on innocent tongues,
My friend, you would not tell with such high zest
To children ardent for some desperate glory,
The old Lie; Dulce et Decorum est
Pro patria mori.

WILFRED OWEN, 1893–1918

# EXPLORERS

'In fourteen hundred and ninety two, Columbus sailed the ocean blue.' He was a hopeless explorer. He reached America by accident. Believing it to be an island, he named it Santa Isla. Honestly, the man was an idiot.

❖

In 1770 Captain Cook discovered Australia, to the enormous surprise of the Aborigines.

❖

In 1840 Captain William Hobson declared British sovereignty over the whole of New Zealand. When a French frigate for the Nanto-Bordelaise trading company arrived two months later, they were too late. Hobson later became New Zealand's first governor.

❖

Sir Walter Raleigh, courtier and explorer, brought tobacco back to England from the American state of Virginia in 1586. It would become a major cash crop. There is a story that when Raleigh's servant first saw him smoking it, he threw a bucket of water over his master to 'put him out'. Raleigh is also credited with bringing potatoes to England and Ireland for the first time, though this may be apocryphal.

In 1863 British explorers John Hanning Speke and J. A. Grant announced that they had found the source of the river Nile, astounding the people living there.

❖

Edmund Hilary and Tenzing Norgay reached the summit of Everest on 29 May 1953. Interestingly, Everest is not the biggest mountain on earth if you take the height from top to bottom. The actual highest mountain is Hawaii, though, to be fair, most of it is underwater, which hampers even serious climbers.

### Oddities

The Rosetta stone was found by a French army engineer. It was taken by the British and transported to London. Before the find, hieroglyphics were a mystery. Luckily, the Ptolemaic dynasty of Alexandria had descended from one of Alexander the Great's generals, Ptolemy. As a result, the stone was marked with a Greek translation and so hieroglyphics were understood for the first time. The phrase 'Rosetta stone' has come to mean anything that provides a key to sudden, illuminating understanding.

In 1607 Captain John Smith landed with colonists in Virginia (named for the Virgin Queen, Elizabeth I), establishing the first permanent settlement.

Howard Carter and Lord Carnarvon finally opened the tomb of King Tutankhamun in the Valley of Kings, Egypt, in 1922. It was a slow, painstaking process and it was months before they laid eyes on the inner tomb, containing the famous gold sarcophagus of the young Pharaoh and many other items of incredible value and antiquity.

### Oddities

Flavius Romulus Augustus was deposed by the Germanic chieftain Odoacer in AD 467. Romulus Augustus was the last of the Western Roman emperors, so this date is sometimes given as the end of the Roman Empire, though the Eastern Roman Empire around Constantinople survived for centuries after this date.

Richard Francis Burton, an extraordinary character by anyone's standards, was born in 1821. As well as a successful army career, in which he served in India as a captain, he travelled in disguise to Mecca, aided in the deception by an astonishing command of more than twenty languages and dialects, including Hindustani, Gujerati, Persian and Arabic. He had himself circumcised so that he would not be given away. He was a consul in Damascus, a spy, a superb fencer and a man often at odds with the moral aspect of Victorian society. Later, he went on to explore much of Africa and translate a number of risqué works, including *The Kama Sutra*, *Arabian Nights*, *The Perfumed Garden* and others. He once said he was proud to have committed every sin in the Ten Commandments.

### To Remember the Days in a Month

*Thirty days hath September,*
*April, June and November*
*All the rest have 31 days clear*
*Except February alone*
*Which has but 28, but 29 in each leap year.*

## The Soldier

If I should die, think only this of me:
  That there's some corner of a foreign field
That is for ever England. There shall be
  In that rich earth a richer dust concealed;
A dust whom England bore, shaped, made aware,
  Gave, once, her flowers to love, her ways to roam,
A body of England's, breathing English air,
  Washed by the rivers, blest by suns of home.
And think, this heart, all evil shed away,
  A pulse in the eternal mind, no less
Gives somewhere back the thoughts by England given;
  Her sights and sounds; dreams happy as her day;
And laughter, learnt of friends; and gentleness,
  In hearts at peace, under an English heaven.

Rupert Brooke, 1887–1915

FESTIVALS

NEW YEAR'S DAY
1 January

TWELFTH NIGHT
5 January

THREE KINGS
6 January

CANDLEMAS DAY
2 February

ST VALENTINE'S DAY
14 February

ST DAVID'S DAY
1 March

ST PATRICK'S DAY
17 March

LADY DAY
25 March

ALL FOOL'S DAY
1 April

ST GEORGE'S DAY AND
SHAKESPEARE'S BIRTHDAY
23 April

ASCENSION DAY
30 May

MIDSUMMER DAY
21 June

St Swithin's Day
15 July

Battle of Britain Day
15 September

Michealmas
24 September

Trafalgar Day
21 October

All Hallow's Eve
31 October

Remembrance Day
11 November

St Andrew's Day
30 November

St Nicolas'
(Santa Claus') Day
6 December

Christmas Day
25 December

St Stephen's Day and
Boxing Day
26 December

## NATURE

These are the days when birds come back,
A very few, a bird or two,
To take a backward look.

These are the days when skies resume
The old, old sophistries of June,
A blue and gold mistake.

Oh, fraud that cannot cheat the bee,
Almost thy plausibility
Induces my belief,

Till ranks of seeds their witness bear,
And softly through the altered air
Hurries a timid leaf!

Oh, sacrament of summer days,
Oh, last communion in the haze,
Permit a child to join,

Thy sacred emblems to partake,
Thy consecrated bread to break,
Taste thine immortal wine!

EMILY DICKINSON, 1830–1886

## Odd Days

The Vernal Equinox falls on 21 March although it sometimes falls on the day before. The earth is tilted in respect to its path around the sun. As a result of the tilt, there are times in the year when the normal hemisphere days are longest – the summer solstice – and shortest – the winter solstice. The halfway points are known as equinoxes – days of equal light and dark. The Vernal equinox is also known as the feast of Ostara, a pagan goddess of fertility. The words East and Easter are derived from her name, as is oestrogen, the female hormone.

Midsummer's Day, or Summer Solstice – 21 June – is the longest day of the year in Britain. In Australia this is the shortest day of the year. Traditionally it is the festival of the Oak King.

Midwinter's Day or the winter solstice – 21 December – is the shortest day in Britain. It is also known as the festival of the Holly King,

# ASSASSINATIONS

Mahatma Gandhi was killed in New Delhi in 1948 by a Hindu radical.

❖

John F. Kennedy, the thirty-fifth President of the United States, was killed in Dallas, Texas, on 22 November 1963. Lee Harvey Oswald was named as his killer, though there are many conspiracy theories even to this day.

On 15 March, known as the Ides of March, in 44 BC, Julius Caesar was assassinated in Pompey's theatre, Rome.

Archduke Franz Ferdinand was assassinated at Sarajevo in 1914, beginning a domino sequence of events that ended in World War I.

Edward II was murdered in Berkeley Castle in 1327, after attempts to starve and poison him had failed. The final attempt method involved a red-hot poker being inserted where it doesn't show.

Prime Minister Spencer Perceval was assassinated in 1812. Unlike American Presidents, he is the only British Prime Minister to date to be killed in this way. Perceval's assassin, John Bellingham, was later hanged.

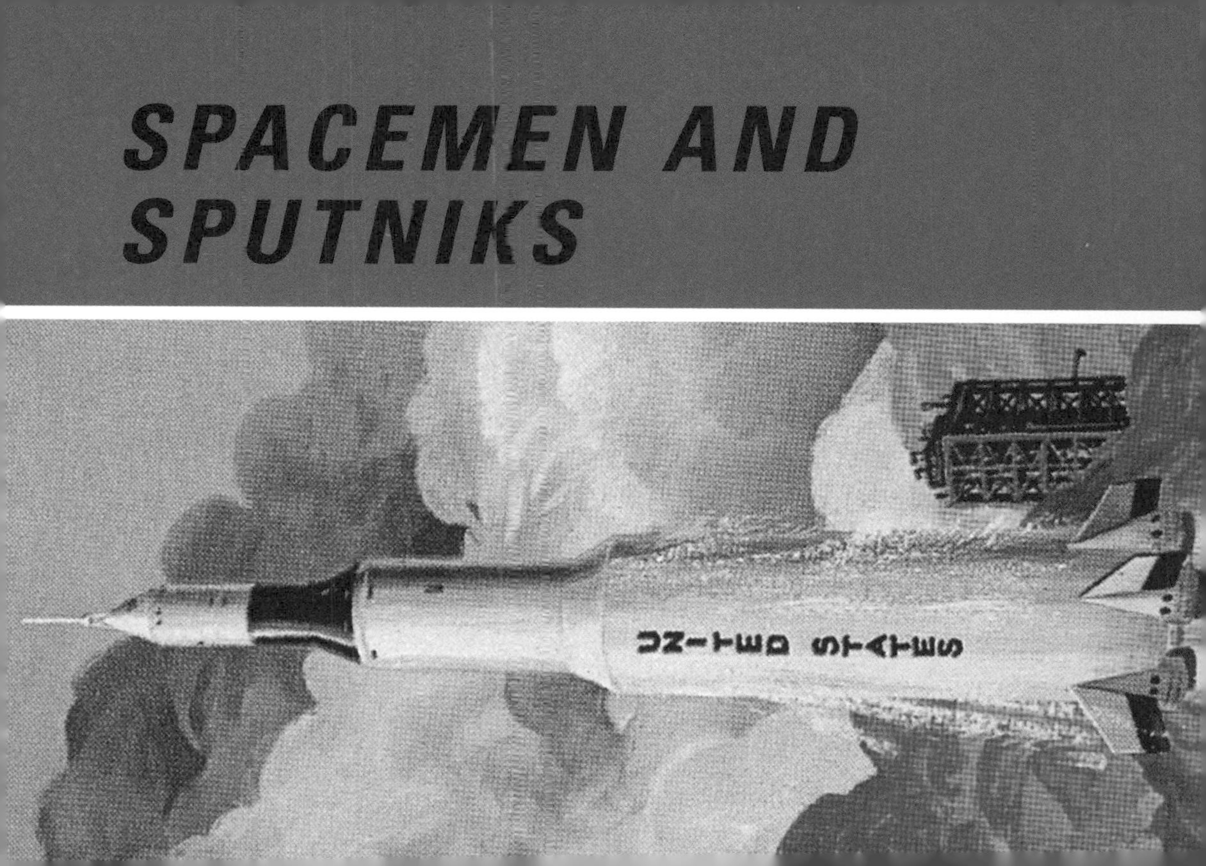
SPACEMEN AND
SPUTNIKS
UNITED STATES

The first space satellite, *Sputnik 1*, was launched by the Soviet Union in 1957. Along with the first probe to Venus, the first man and woman in space and the first moon probe, this was the beginning of a period of incredible achievement that forced America to catch up.

❖

The USSR launched the *Sputnik 2* space mission in 1957, carrying the first dog in space, Laika. She did not survive the trip.

❖

In 1959 the unmanned Soviet probe *Luna 2* crashed into the moon. It was the first human machine to reach the surface, with a hard landing that destroyed *Luna 2* in the process.

❖

In 1961 the cosmonaut Yuri Gagarin became the first man in space, orbiting the earth for 108 minutes and travelling at 17,000 miles an hour, so that he also became the fastest man alive.

USA
USA

In 1963 Valentina Tereshkova became the first woman in space on the mission *Vostok 6*. She made 48 orbits of the earth and was up there for 71 hours.

❖

The first soft landing of an unmanned probe on the moon was achieved by the USSR in 1966. The probe was named *Luna 9*. This Soviet success spurred America on in the race to put a man on the moon. A previous American probe, *Ranger 8*, crashed into the moon in 1965, as it was designed to do, sending back 7,000 pictures before impact. However, the soft landing of *Luna 9* showed that one day a manned landing might be possible.

❖

An explosion on board the *Apollo 13* resulted in the famous, oft-misquoted message: 'Houston, we've had a problem.'

Alan Shepard became the first American in space in the *Freedom 7* mission flight into orbit, part of the Mercury series of flights that would be followed by the famous Gemini and Apollo missions. He reached space only a month behind Yuri Gagarin.

He played golf on the moon in 1971, at the end of the *Apollo 14* mission, hitting the ball 'miles and miles and miles'. It was the longest golf drive in history until 22 November 2006, when Russian Cosmonaut Mikhail Tyurin hit one from the International Space Station. That ball is still orbiting.

❖

The first Briton – Helen Sharman – reached space in 1991 with the Soviet craft *Soyuz TM-12*, launched from Kazakhstan. Astonishingly, she answered an advert that said 'Astronaut wanted. No experience necessary' and was selected from more than 13,000 applicants. Technically, she is a cosmonaut as it was a Russian operation. Sharman took a photograph of the Queen with her as well as a passport in case she landed outside Russia.

In 2001 the Russian space station *Mir* was moved into a decaying orbit and burnt up over the Pacific Ocean near Fiji. The flaming pieces were visible to the naked eye.

❖

Billionaire Dennis Tito became the first space tourist in 2001, with a trip to the International Space Station. The Americans only allowed the flight when he promised to pay for anything he broke.

## Oddities

Income tax was introduced in Britain for the first time in 1798, as a 'temporary measure' to raise funds to fight the French in the Napoleonic wars. The Prime Minister, William Pitt, admitted that the idea was 'repugnant to the customs and manners of the nation' but went ahead regardless. The crisis with France passed and the law was repealed in 1816. Unfortunately, the tax raised so much money for the government that they were unlikely to forget such a good wheeze, reintroducing income tax in 1842.

# EXTRAORDINARY MOMENTS

In 1215 the Magna Carta was reluctantly sealed by King John. It limited the absolute power of the king and gave more power to his barons. Clause 39 had a wider application than they anticipated and became a fundamental precept of British law: 'No freeman shall be arrested or imprisoned or dispossessed or outlawed or banished or in any way molested, nor will we go upon him, nor send upon him, except by lawful judgement of his peers and the law of the land.'

❖

In 1381 the Peasants Revolt broke out. The rebellion was led by Walter 'Wat' Tyler, Jack Straw and John Ball, a renegade priest, and was widespread in the east of England, with 'The Men of Essex' joining factions from Kent and other places. The uprising was due to a new poll tax. It resulted in an attack on the Tower of London, the murder of both the Lord Chancellor and the Archbishop of Canterbury and the destruction of the Savoy Palace.

The Peasants Revolt was crushed at Smithfield and St John's Fields, London. King Richard II reneged on promises made to the rebels. They were betrayed, captured and tortured, the rebellion was broken and the poll tax levied.

In 1776 the Declaration of Independence was made by the United States, separating from Britain after more than a year of war. It is still known as 'Independence Day' in the US. The war went on for another seven years until 1783. In that year, Cornwallis, the English military commander, hoped to escape a tightening noose of American forces. He was prevented from doing so by a French naval blockade. Famously, his military band played 'The World Turned Upside Down' as he surrendered. To celebrate their part in the war, the French later gave the Statue of Liberty to America.

### Odd Days

Shrove Tuesday, better known as Pancake Day, came from the attempt to use up all the food you weren't allowed to eat in Lent on the night before Lent began. The word 'shrove' is the past tense of 'shrive', which means confessing one's sins, so as to go into Lent with a spotless soul. With a little lemon and sugar, batter pancakes are delicious and well worth the effort. It is absolutely crucial that you try to flip one. They have been landing on floors and sticking to ceilings for centuries.

In 1872 the *Mary Celeste* was found adrift, one of the great mysteries of history. Having sailed from New York on 7 November of that year, the ship was found without a soul aboard. There is some evidence of the crew leaving in a great hurry, abandoning their pipes and boots. Sir Arthur Conan Doyle would later explore the mystery in a short story, bringing it to popular attention.

In 1917 the Russian revolution began, leading to the abdication of Tsar Nicholas II on 16 March and his execution along with his family. From these grim events, the USSR formed. It lasted for 74 years, until 1991.

1929 saw the Wall Street Crash. Investors panicked, selling shares. The US stock market collapsed, bringing in a decade of mass unemployment and poverty for millions.

In 1940 the bombing of Coventry took place. After breakthroughs decrypting the German Enigma code machine, Churchill had advance warning of the attack and could have evacuated the city. If he had done so, he would have revealed that the Allies had broken the code. Churchill made a bitterly hard decision and did not warn the city. Up to 1,000 people died and Coventry was all but destroyed. The Germans remained unaware that their Enigma code had been cracked until the end of the war. Many more lives were saved as a result, but it is still one of those times when few people would have liked to be in Churchill's shoes, faced with that decision.

1944 witnessed the bombing of Nuremburg. Ninety-seven planes and crews from Bomber Command were lost in one night. More airmen were killed in this single attack than in the Battle of Britain.

❖

In 1944 the Liberation of Paris by French forces took place. France was actually liberated from the Nazis by American, Canadian and British forces. The French leader, De Gaulle, spent the war in London, but insisted on being the first into Paris and was greeted with great joy on the day. He was also greeted with sniper fire from German soldiers and French fascists, but he was not hurt and American soldiers moved in quickly to mop up the last of the resistance.

❖

1945 saw the liberation of Auschwitz by the Soviet army.

In 1945 American forces liberated the concentration camp of Dachau. The soldiers were so appalled at what they saw that they executed the commandant and 500 of his troops.

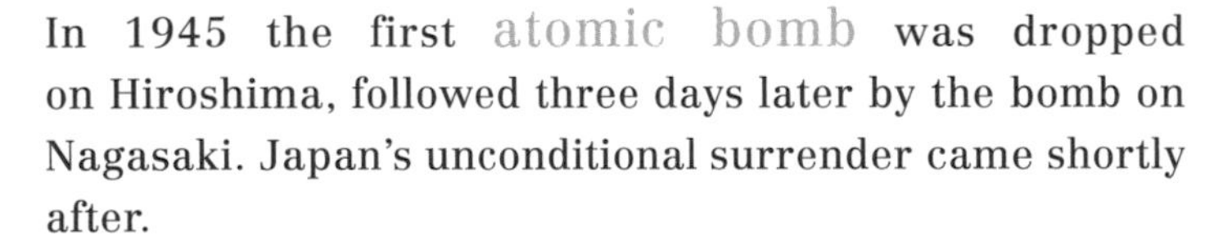

In 1945 the first atomic bomb was dropped on Hiroshima, followed three days later by the bomb on Nagasaki. Japan's unconditional surrender came shortly after.

In 1969 Neil Armstrong stepped onto the moon surface in the Sea of Tranquillity, saying, 'One small step for man, one giant leap for mankind.' Recently, it has been suggested that he did say 'a man' as he intended to, but the extra word was lost in a poor signal. Fair enough. The moon was further away than we had ever been before, after all. Buzz Aldrin followed him, and Michael Collins was the third member of the team, remaining on board.

In 1975 the war in Vietnam ended as Saigon surrendered to the Viet Cong.

In 1980 the SAS stormed the Iranian embassy to save 26 hostages from six terrorists protesting at the rule of the Ayatollah Khomeini. The SAS rescued all 26 in eleven minutes, killing five of the terrorists and capturing the sixth.

In 1990 French and British engineers met in the middle of the Channel Tunnel for the first time. At 31 miles long, the tunnel is considered to be one of the wonders of the modern world.

◆

On 11 September 2001 two planes were flown into the World Trade Centre by Islamic extremists, killing around 3,000 people and causing the Twin Towers to collapse. The United States declared war on terror as a result.

### Oddities

Elvis Presley starred in 30 successful films and made 81 albums, all of which went from gold (500,000 copies sold) to triple triple platinum (9 million sold). From those, 53 singles were taken, with similar sales. He is the most successful recording artist in history by a huge margin. He died of a heart attack induced by barbiturates at his home in Memphis.

## To Autumn

1.

SEASON of mists and mellow fruitfulness,
  Close bosom-friend of the maturing sun;
Conspiring with him how to load and bless
  With fruit the vines that round the thatch-eves run;
To bend with apples the moss'd cottage-trees,
  And fill all fruit with ripeness to the core;
To swell the gourd, and plump the hazel shells
With a sweet kernel; to set budding more,
  And still more, later flowers for the bees,
  Until they think warm days will never cease,
  For Summer has o'er-brimm'd their clammy cells.

2.

Who hath not seen thee oft amid thy store?
  Sometimes whoever seeks abroad may find
Thee sitting careless on a granary floor,
  Thy hair soft-lifted by the winnowing wind;
Or on a half-reap'd furrow sound asleep,
  Drows'd with the fume of poppies, while thy hook

Spares the next swath and all its twined flowers:
And sometimes like a gleaner thou dost keep
Steady thy laden head across a brook;
Or by a cyder-press, with patient look,
Thou watchest the last oozings hours by hours.

3.

Where are the songs of Spring? Ay, where are they?
Think not of them, thou hast thy music too, –
While barred clouds bloom the soft-dying day,
And touch the stubble plains with rosy hue;
Then in a wailful choir the small gnats mourn
Among the river sallows, borne aloft
Or sinking as the light wind lives or dies;
And full-grown lambs loud bleat from hilly bourn;
Hedge-crickets sing; and now with treble soft
The red-breast whistles from a garden-croft;
And gathering swallows twitter in the skies.

John Keats, 1795–1821

ROYAL STORIES

Canute was the King of all England, Denmark, Norway and bits of Sweden. His useless sons lost the lot after his death in 1035. Interestingly, the famous story about him holding back the waves has two versions. In one, his courtiers flattered him and he became arrogant enough to think he could hold back the tide – failing miserably. In the other, to demonstrate to those same courtiers that even a king has limits, he showed that he could not hold back the tide. Given that the man was fantastically able and cunning, the latter story is probably the true version. He is buried in Winchester.

❖

Elizabeth I, daughter of Henry VIII and Anne Boleyn, was imprisoned while her sister Mary ruled. She came to power in 1558 when Mary died without heirs. The fact that neither sister had children is sometimes seen as evidence that their father Henry may have had syphilis, which sometimes leads to barren children. Elizabeth formally ratified the Church of England in 1563. From that point, English Catholics were persecuted with almost as much fervour as Mary had persecuted the Protestants before.

William III died after his horse stumbled on a mole-hill at Hampton Court. So today Catholics in Ireland raise a toast to 'the little men in velvet jackets' – the moles responsible for his demise. As William III had no heirs, the line passed to Queen Anne, his sister-in-law, daughter of James II and Anne Hyde. When she too died without heirs, after seventeen children died in infancy and one dying aged eleven from 'too much dancing', the Hanoverian line began with George I.

Henry V was crowned at Westminster Abbey, the ablest of the English medieval warrior kings. He went on to win the Battle of Agincourt in 1415, reconquered Normandy, of which he was Duke, and married the daughter of the King of France, titling himself king of that country.

### Oddities

Around 1745 the national anthem *God Save the King* was sung for the first time in London theatres. The relevant King was George II.

Richard III was the last English king to die on the battlefield. His defeat bought the Tudors to power in the form of Henry VII. Richard's later reputation suffered through Tudor propaganda and the image of a cruel hunchback created by William Shakespeare. His famous hump could have been no more than the mass of muscle that comes from fighting with a broadsword. At the Battle of Bosworth Field, Richard refused to run, bellowing out these final words: 'I will die King of England.'

❖

Henry VIII's daughters were declared illegitimate in 1536, on his order, to allow the children of his latest wife, Jane Seymour, to inherit. Sadly, she died giving birth to her son, Edward, after a caesarean without anaesthetic. Though he survived to be king, Edward VI died aged only 15, leaving the throne to be contested and then taken by Mary and Elizabeth in turn.

❖

The consecration of Westminster Abbey in London took place in 1065. The first king to be crowned there was Harold II, who went on to lose the Battle of Hastings. The next king to be crowned there was William I, better known as William the Conqueror.

**George III** was the first of the Hanoverian line to actually be born in England, at Norfolk House, London. He was also the first to speak fluent English. Due to his love of agriculture, he was popularly known as 'Farmer George'.

❖

**Edward I** ended hopes of Welsh independence by making his son 'Prince of Wales'. Legend has it that he promised the Welsh a ruler who would speak no English – then produced the infant son. He built huge castles in Wales before moving on to subdue Scotland, led at that time by Robert the Bruce and the famous rebel William Wallace. Edward's final command to his son, Edward II, was to boil the flesh from his bones and carry the bones in every battle against the Scots until they were destroyed. His son went on to lose the Battle of Bannockburn.

### Odd Days

Oak-Apple, Royal Oak or Acorn Day, 29 May, commemorates the time when King Charles II had to hide in an oak tree to escape his enemies.

Richard the Lionheart was born at Beaumont Palace in Oxford in 1157. He is perhaps most famous for spending less than a year of his ten-year reign in England, spending the rest of the time on Crusades or imprisoned. It is not too surprising that his brother John tried to displace this absentee king. The story of Robin Hood comes from this period.

❖

George I was crowned in Westminster Abbey in 1714. The Protestant Hanoverian came to the throne despite George hardly even being able to speak the language, because of the Act of Settlement in 1701 which forbade any future Catholic monarch. His inheritance came through his wife Sophia who was a granddaughter of James I.

❖

Harold Godwinson was crowned King of England in January 1066. He was later killed at the Battle of Hastings in October, after killing his brother Tostig at the Battle of Stamford Bridge. At Hastings he was shot in the eye and then had to hold still for hours while the Bayeux Tapestry people finished their scene.

Edward III, son of Edward II and grandson of Edward I, was one of the most successful kings in English history. He was there at the beginning of the Hundred Years' War and won the naval Battle of Sluys as well as the more famous Crécy in 1346. He became King of France as well, in 1340, and his successors kept Calais until it was lost by Mary I's Spanish husband in 1558.

❖

Athelstan was the first king of England. He died in 939 and was buried in Malmesbury Abbey.

❖

Charles I, King of Great Britain and Ireland, was born in 1600. He entered into a struggle against parliamentary power and ruled without them for eleven years. The Royalists (Cavaliers) and Parliamentarians (Roundheads) fought the English Civil War, which Charles lost. He was executed on 30 January 1649. Attempts to rule without a king eventually failed after Oliver Cromwell's death, and Charles I's son was invited to take the throne in 1660 – a period known as 'The Restoration'. Unfortunately for the succession, Charles II has three stillborn legitimate children and almost twenty illegitimate ones. His brother James II inherited the throne on his death.

In 1917, embarrassed by family links to Germany in the middle of a war with them, King George V changed his surname from Saxe-Coburg-Gotha to Windsor, after the castle.

Edmund I, 'The Magnificent', was crowned at Kingston-upon-Thames. He defeated the Norse King of York, Olaf Guthfrithson, and the Britons of Strathclyde. He was buried in Glastonbury Abbey.

### Six Wives of King Henry VIII

*Divorced, beheaded, died,*
*Divorced, beheaded, survived.*

**Catherine of Aragon** (the divorce began the establishment of the Church of England)
**Anne Boleyn**
**Jane Seymour** (dies in childbirth, mother of the only son)
**Anne of Cleves**
**Catherine Howard**
**Catherine Parr**

On 11 December 1936 Edward VIII abdicated. Part of his speech was drafted by Winston Churchill. His brother George VI – the father of Elizabeth II – became king. George VI was a shy man with a stammer who had never expected to become king. He ruled throughout World War II, refusing to leave London during the Blitz.

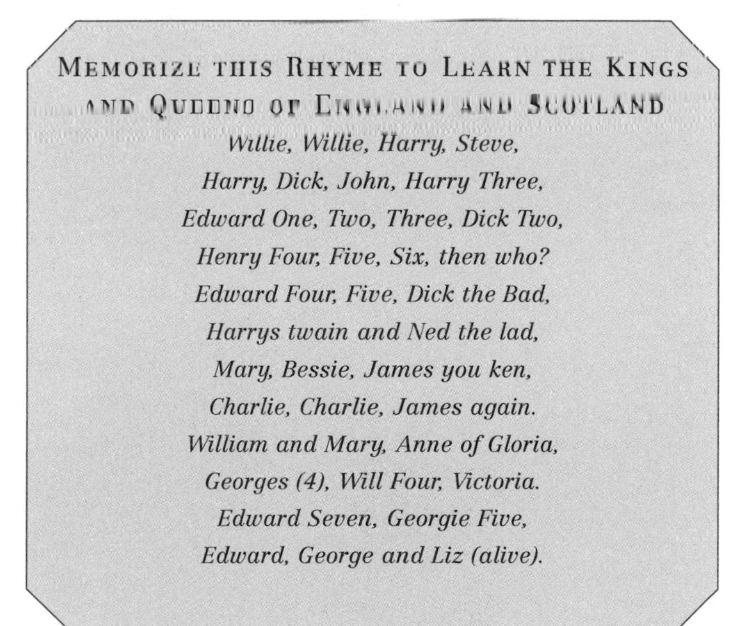

MEMORIZE THIS RHYME TO LEARN THE KINGS AND QUEENS OF ENGLAND AND SCOTLAND

*Willie, Willie, Harry, Steve,*
*Harry, Dick, John, Harry Three,*
*Edward One, Two, Three, Dick Two,*
*Henry Four, Five, Six, then who?*
*Edward Four, Five, Dick the Bad,*
*Harrys twain and Ned the lad,*
*Mary, Bessie, James you ken,*
*Charlie, Charlie, James again.*
*William and Mary, Anne of Gloria,*
*Georges (4), Will Four, Victoria.*
*Edward Seven, Georgie Five,*
*Edward, George and Liz (alive).*

# INTERESTING SAINTS

14 February is St Valentine's Day. It evolved from 'Lupercalia', a racy festival in the Roman calendar where pretty much anything was allowed. St Valentine was a priest who married Christian couples and so disobeyed the Roman emperor, who had forbidden soldiers to marry. Valentine was beheaded on this day in AD 270 or 271.

❖

1 March is St David's Day. The Patron Saint of Wales, St David is known there as 'Dewi Sant' or St Daveth. Legend has it that he was the uncle of King Arthur. He is also said to be the one who came up with a leek as a Welsh symbol, to distinguish their soldiers on the battlefield.

### Odd Days

Lady Day is on 25 March. It is also the day of the Annunciation of Mary the Virgin and the feast day of Dismas, the patron saint of condemned prisoners. It is one of the four official 'Quarter Days' in England that divided up the year. As well as being Christian festivals, rent became due on these days, a practice still continued today in some parts.

30 March is the feast day of Joan of Arc, the patron saint of France. She fought the English, was burned at the stake and had her ashes thrown into the Seine by the English so no relics could be taken. She died in 1431.

❖

16 April is famously the feast of Saint Bernadette, a frail asthmatic who made Lourdes a place of pilgrimage for millions after seeing visions of the Virgin Mary there.

❖

25 May is the saint day of Mary Magdalen dei Pazzi. The Three Marys are Mary Magdalen, Mary the wife of Cleophas (mentioned in the gospel of John) and Mary the mother of James.

❖

29 June is the feast day of St Peter the apostle, who is meant to hold the keys to heaven. He is the patron saint of butchers, bakers and clock makers. His bones are in St Peter's Church in Rome.

15 July is St Swithin's Day. When St Swithin's bones were moved to a shrine in Winchester Cathedral on this day in AD 971, it rained for the next forty days.

❖

25 July marks the feast day of St Christopher. The Vatican removed this feast day from the official list in 1969, which is a bit of a shame. St Christopher was said to be an enormously strong Roman named Reprobus. Reprobus asked a Christian hermit how he could serve Jesus. The man directed him to a fast-flowing stream, where Reprobus met a child asking to be carried across. The child became heavier and heavier, revealing that he was the child Jesus and his weight was the weight of the sins of the world. The boy then baptised Reprobus in the river, naming him 'Christopher', which means 'Christ-Carrier' in Greek. Despite his drop in official status, Christopher is still the patron saint of travellers and lorry drivers. In some parts of England it is believed that seeing his image protects you against sudden or accidental death.

❖

22 July is the saint's day of Mary Magdalen who was present at the crucifixion and at the tomb, finding it empty. She is the patron of repentant sinners.

31 July marks the feast day of Ignatius of Loyola, a Spanish soldier who was badly wounded in the siege of Pamplona. During his long convalescence he became converted and together with a small group of followers resolved to form a new religious order. The Society of Jesus agreed to strict vows of obedience, to go anywhere on the Pope's orders and to concentrate particularly on teaching the young and uneducated.

❖

7 August is the feast day of Dominic, who founded the Dominican Order, known as the Black Friars, in 1215. He was much involved in the struggle against the Cathars.

❖

29 August is the feast day of John the Baptist. This marks the day when he was beheaded on the orders of Herod, with his head, as requested, presented on a dish to Salome.

Michaelmas – 29 September – is Archangel Michael's feast day and traditionally the third English Quarter Day, when rents become due. Michael is the patron saint of artists, police officers, soldiers and grocers. He is a very martial angel indeed and carries a sword and a pair of scales to weigh souls.

❖

29 September is also the feast of the Archangel Gabriel, who brought a message to Mary. As a result, the angel is patron saint of postmen. It used to be in March but sometimes the post is delayed.

Jerome, whose feast day is 30 September, was the translator of the Bible from Hebrew and Greek into Latin, a celebrated scholar and author. He moved around the Middle East from Palestine to Rome to Constantinople, finally dying in Bethlehem in AD 420.

❖

Elthelburga of Barking's feast day is 11 October (who could resist such a name?). She was the abbess of Barking abbey, possibly a royal princess, and is frequently mentioned in the Venerable Bede's writings.

❖

Teresa of Avila's feast day is 11 October. A reformer and Carmelite nun, she was the first woman to be named a Doctor at the Church.

❖

13 October marks the feast day of Edward the Confessor, king of England during the eleventh century.

❖

19 October is the feast day of Frideswide, daughter of a Mercian lord whose abbey was the nucleus of the city of Oxford. She is also the patron saint of the city.

Luke was an evangelist, friend of Paul and gospel writer, and his feast day is celebrated on 18 October.

❖

November begins with the Church festivals of All Saints and All Souls. On All Souls, Catholics believe that reciting six 'Our Fathers', six 'Hail Marys' and six 'Glory be to the Fathers' will free a single soul from Purgatory into Heaven.

### Oddities

John Lennon died in New York, having been shot by a fan. His murderer, Mark Chapman, is still in prison. Chapman carried a copy of *Catcher in the Rye*, which has become part of the mythology around that book. In any survey of reading habits of psychopathic killers, *Catcher in the Rye* always tops the list.

As with any great artist, the personal tragedy is only part of the loss. Though Lennon's relationship with Paul McCartney was occasionally rocky, they were beginning to be reconciled. There is a good chance they would have resumed the greatest music-writing partnership of the twentieth century.

11 November is St Martin's Day or 'Martinmas'. Originally a Roman soldier, Saint Martin converted to Christianity and refused to fight, later becoming a monk, then a bishop in Gaul. Traditionally, it is also the last Scottish Quarter Day, when rents become due and all manner of official business is conducted.

❖

21 December is the feast day of Thomas. The apostle was both criticized and celebrated for his scepticism, hence 'doubting Thomas'.

### Odd Days

Easter will come either at the end of March or in April. A movable feast, it occurs on the first Sunday after the Paschal full moon – the full moon that occurs on the vernal equinox or during the 28 days after it. Easter is by far the most important Christian festival, and one ancient tradition has it that the sun dances on Easter Sunday morning. If you stay up till dawn to test this theory, it is also important to remember not to stare directly at it. Eyesight is more important than dancing suns.

## The Charge of the Light Brigade

Half a league, half a league,
  Half a league onward,
All in the valley of Death
  Rode the six hundred.
'Forward the Light Brigade!
Charge for the guns!' he said.
Into the valley of Death
  Rode the six hundred.

'Forward, the Light Brigade!'
Was there a man dismay'd?
Not tho' the soldier knew
  Someone had blunder'd.
Theirs not to make reply,
Theirs not to reason why,
Theirs but to do and die.
Into the valley of Death
  Rode the six hundred.

Cannon to right of them,
Cannon to left of them,
Cannon in front of them
  Volley'd and thunder'd;
Storm'd at with shot and shell,
Boldly they rode and well,
Into the jaws of Death,
Into the mouth of hell
  Rode the six hundred.

Flash'd all their sabres bare,
Flash'd as they turn'd in air
Sabring the gunners there,
Charging an army, while
  All the world wonder'd.
Plunged in the battery-smoke
Right thro' the line they broke;
Cossack and Russian
Reel'd from the sabre-stroke
  Shatter'd and sunder'd.

Then they rode back, but not,
  Not the six hundred.

Cannon to right of them,
Cannon to left of them,
Cannon behind them
  Volley'd and thunder'd;
Storm'd at with shot and shell,
While horse and hero fell,
They that had fought so well
Came thro' the jaws of Death,
Back from the mouth of Hell,
All that was left of them,
  Left of six hundred.

When can their glory fade?
O the wild charge they made!
  All the world wonder'd.
Honour the charge they made!
Honour the Light Brigade,
  Noble six hundred!

ALFRED TENNYSON, 1809–1892

DISCOVERIES

North Cache
North Cove
Arms
Spring
ye
Spye glass
Hill
Bulk of
Treasure
here
Swamp
the
Groves
Stream
Stockade
White Rock
Skeleton Island

Sir Joseph John Thomson was born near Manchester. In 1856 he discovered the existence of the electron. He also pioneered mass spectrometry and discovered the existence of isotopes of elements. He won the Nobel Prize for Physics in 1906.

❖

James Prescott Joule was the first to demonstrate that heat is a form of energy and his work became the basis for the theory of conservation of energy. With Lord Kelvin, he did groundbreaking work on temperatures and formulated the absolute scale. The unit of energy, 'joule', is named after him, just as the absolute-zero scale is named after Kelvin.

❖

Anders Celsius, a Swedish astronomer, was born in 1701. He is best known for the creation of the Celsius temperature scale, which sets the melting point of ice at zero degrees and the boiling point of water at 100 degrees. It is also known as 'Centigrade' – meaning a scale of 100 degrees. Alternatively, temperature can be measured in Kelvin, from absolute zero, or Fahrenheit, which originally used human body temperature as the 100-degree mark. Lack of accurate testing meant that human body temperature is actually 98.4 degrees on the Fahrenheit scale.

Alexander Fleming was the discoverer of penicillin, the first general-purpose antibiotic. Others claim to have discovered it first, but history can be hard on the losers. Fleming died in 1955 and is buried in St Paul's Cathedral. Few lives have saved so many others.

In 1610 Galileo discovered the four largest moons orbiting Jupiter, still known today as the Galilean moons.

Henry Maudslay is an almost forgotten name of British engineering history. He invented the first bench micrometer capable of measuring one ten-thousandth of an inch and became an expert in industrial machinery, developing the precision screw-cutting lathe. He completed huge commissions for Marc Isambard Brunel, father of the more famous Isambard Kingdom Brunel. He also trained many men who made great strides in engineering themselves, including Joseph Clement, who produced the precision machinery for Charles Babbage's 'difference engine', and James Nasmyth, who invented the steam hammer and created machine tools for Brunel's ship the *SS Great Britain*.

The astronomer Nicolaus Copernicus was born in 1473. His groundbreaking understanding of the solar system overturned the idea that the universe revolves around the earth. It seems a little obvious now, but he was the first to describe the planets spinning around the sun.

Joseph Lister is the 'Father of antiseptic surgery'. His work, in conjunction with that of Louis Pasteur and the Hungarian doctor Ignaz Semmelweis, dramatically lowered death rates after surgery in British hospitals. Lister found that spraying a constant mist of carbolic acid over a wound and his own hands prevented sepsis. The drawback was that the skin of his hands became inflamed by constant exposure to the acid.

## To Remember the Notes on a Musical Stave

Notes on the lines of the treble clef:
Every Good Boy Deserves a Favour

Notes between the lines of the treble clef stave:
Furry Animals Cook Excellently

Notes on the lines of the bass stave:
Good Boys Do Fine Always

Notes between the lines of the bass stave:
All Cows Eat Grass

The theoretical physicist Paul Dirac, born in Bristol in 1902, was one of the founders of the field of quantum physics and formulated the 'Dirac equation', which predicted the existence of anti-matter in the universe. He won the Nobel Prize for Physics in 1933, sharing it with Erwin Schrödinger, a man most famous for his question about a cat in a box.

❖

Alfred Nobel demonstrated dynamite for the first time in 1867 in a Surrey quarry. Although the explosive is based on nitroglycerin, the huge advantage it has over that substance is that it could be roughly handled or even dropped without going off. Nobel combined nitroglycerin with clay and a pinch of sodium carbonate, forming the mixture into short sticks with fuses. Later in life, he used his fortune to endow the Nobel prizes.

❖

Francis Crick, together with James Watson and Maurice Wilkins, discovered the DNA helix. The three men shared the Nobel Prize for Physiology or Medicine in 1962.

Pluto was discovered by American astronomer Clyde Tombaugh in 1930. Even today the argument rages about whether it can be classed as a planet. It does not orbit the sun on the same plane as the other planets, sometimes even coming closer in than Neptune, the eighth planet. However, Pluto is big enough to be spherical (as opposed to irregularly shaped asteroids) and it also has a moon, 'Charon'. We think it's a planet.

❖

In 1846 Neptune was discovered by German astronomer Johann Galle. Neptune is the eighth planet from the sun, with only Pluto outside it.

❖

James Watt developed and improved early types of steam engine, creating the form that would become the workhorse of the world. He was the first to use the term 'horsepower' and the unit of power, a 'watt', is named after him. He died in 1819.

Dolly, the world's first cloned sheep, was born in 1996, though her existence was kept secret until February 1997. In fact, previous clones had been created from embryonic cells, but Dolly was the first mammal to be created from adult cells. In theory, Elvis could be reborn in the same way.

❖

Michael Faraday, known as the 'Father of Electricity', was born in London. He went on to discover electromagnetic induction and the laws of electrolysis. He was also the first to isolate benzene and to synthesise chlorocarbons. In 1831 he demonstrated the production of electricity from an induction ring. One of the great experimental scientists, he discovered that a copper disc rotating between the poles of a horseshoe magnet could produce a current on wires through the disc. This led to the first electrical transformer and the first electric motor. A genius of the first order.

Sir William Ramsay won the Nobel Prize for Chemistry in 1904 for discovering the noble gases argon, neon, krypton and xenon. He was also the first person to isolate helium.

Isaac Newton was born in Lincolnshire in 1643. He became the leading mathematician of the age, formulating laws of motion and a new understanding of light and colour.

Sir Humphry Davy discovered the anaesthetic properties of laughing gas, and the elements potassium, sodium, barium, strontium, magnesium and calcium. He is most famous for devising safety lamps for use in mining.

Sir Francis Beaufort created a scale to measure wind force. His invention, named after him, is still in use today.

# FUNERAL PROCESSIONS AT ST PAUL'S CATHEDRAL

The funeral of Lord Nelson took place at St Paul's Cathedral in 1806. Having been preserved in alcohol for the voyage home, his body had been brought up the Thames the previous day, staying in the Admiralty overnight. The cathedral was hung with enemy banners captured at Trafalgar for the occasion. As the service ends, his coffin was lowered into the crypt, secure in an ebony coffin, where it remains to this day.

❖

The state funeral of Arthur Wellesley, first Duke of Wellington, took place at St Paul's Cathedral in 1850. The interior of the cathedral was covered in black velvet for the occasion and illuminated by gaslight. The gun carriage and coffin of Cornish porphyry weighed seventeen and a half tons and was drawn by bay horses sporting black ostrich plumes. The procession made its way from Chelsea Royal Hospital to the bottom of Ludgate Hill. At this point, the horses were exhausted by the tremendous weight. Men of the Royal Navy stepped forward to take their place and, with ropes, pull the sarcophagus and carriage up the hill to St Paul's. This became the tradition for full state funerals and was re-enacted for Sir Winston Churchill's funeral.

Winston Churchill died in London at the age of 90 on 24 January 1965. St Paul's Cathedral, home to the tombs of Nelson and Wellington, was the venue for Churchill's state funeral six days later, most of which he planned himself.

FUNERAL PROCESSIONS AT ST PAUL'S CATHEDRAL

Also buried in St Paul's are …

Sir Christopher Wren, who died at the age of 91, and was the greatest architect of his time. As well as St Paul's Cathedral, he designed the Monument to the Great Fire of 1666, the Royal Observatory at Greenwich and the library at Trinity College, Cambridge, and more than fifty other churches and secular buildings. He is buried in St Paul's under the words: 'Lector, si monumentum requiris, circumspice.' ('Reader, if you seek his monument, look around you.')

J. M. W. Turner, perhaps Britain's greatest painter, was born in Covent Garden, London, in 1775. He died in Chiswick in 1851 and is also buried in St Paul's Cathedral.

Admiral Nelson and his great friend Admiral Lord Collingwood lie together in the same section of the Undercroft in St Paul's.

## Extract from Paradise Lost Book I

Here at least
We shall be free; th' Almighty hath not built
Here for his envy, will not drive us hence:
Here we may reign secure, and in my choyce
To reign is worth ambition though in Hell:
Better to reign in Hell, then serve in Heav'n.

John Milton, 1698–1874

GREAT
DISASTERS

The Great Fire of London began at a baker's in Pudding Lane on 2 September 1666 and burned for three days. The Royal Exchange, St Paul's Cathedral, prisons, hospitals, schools, bridges, churches and city gates were destroyed, as well as 400 streets and 13,200 houses. Even though there was no organized fire service, astonishingly only nine people died. The one good thing about the fire is that it ended the bubonic plague outbreak of 1665. 'The Monument' was later raised to commemorate the fire, and many of the most important commissions to rebuild London went to Christopher Wren, the greatest architect of the day.

In 1883 the volcano Krakatoa exploded in Indonesia. The resulting tsunami killed many thousands on Java and Sumatra. The resulting ash cloud was so vast that it drifted around the earth and caused particularly vivid sunsets for years afterwards.

After the British retreat from Kabul in Afghanistan in 1874, the sole survivor of 16,000 men, women and children arrived at a British sentry post in Jalalabad on 13 January.

### Oddities

Charles Grey, the second Earl Grey, made popular the flowery blend of tea and bergamot orange oil that still bears his name. The exact origin of the blend is unknown, but it may have been a gift when the Earl was Prime Minister in the 1830s. There is a story that one of Earl Grey's men saved a Chinese Mandarin's son from drowning and the tea was given to him as a result. The tea company Twinings managed to make up a blend from the original and marketed it as Earl Grey's Tea.

The United States introduced Prohibition in 1920, making alcohol illegal. Instead of leading to a more orderly and peaceful society, the ban brought in huge revenues for the Mafia, helping to make organized crime a force in the country.

❖

Nazi Germany under Adolf Hitler invaded Poland on 1 September 1939 with 1.5 million troops. The attack was unprovoked and began World War II, which raged until 1945.

❖

The volcano Vesuvius erupted in southern Italy in AD 79, burying the towns of Pompeii, Herculaneum and Stabiae under hot ash and boiling mud. Pompeii in particular is an extraordinary place to visit. Modern excavations revealed an almost intact ancient city, complete with graffiti, houses of ill-repute, a maze of streets, two theatres and a ring for gladiatorial games. There is nowhere quite like it in the world.

General Galtieri ordered the invasion of the British Falkland Islands, triggering the war in 1982. As the Argentinian troops landed, a local radio presenter was live on air. He did not want to announce it live and instead played 'Strangers in the Night' repeatedly until residents understood. The Argentinians insist on referring to the islands as 'The Malvinas', which makes diplomacy difficult as no one can find them on the map.

The Bay of Pigs invasion of Cuba took place in 1961 American-organized Cuban exiles attempted to overthrow Fidel Castro, but failed.

The Glencoe Massacre took place on 13 February 1692. Thirty-eight Macdonalds were killed by Campbells whom they had taken in as guests. Forty more women and children died of exposure after their homes were burned.

On 15 April 1912, after being struck by an iceberg close to midnight on the 14th, RMS *Titanic* sank on her maiden voyage, with the loss of more than 1,500 lives.

The German 6th Army surrendered at Stalingrad in 1943 after months of some of the most vicious fighting of World War II.

❖

The *SS Lusitania* was sunk by a German submarine off the coast of Ireland in 1915, killing 1,200 men, women and children.

### Odd Days

The last Sunday of August is still sometimes known as 'Plague Sunday', commemorating the extraordinary sacrifice of the village of Eyam (pronounced 'Eem') in Derbyshire. The Black Death of 1665 reached them in September of that year. The local rector, William Mompesson, persuaded the villagers to impose a strict quarantine on Eyam to stop the spread of the disease. They succeeded, and none of the villages around them were touched. In Eyam itself, by the time the plague passed, 260 of 350 families had died.

The pride of the British Navy, the *Hood*, was destroyed by the German battleship Bismarck, just after six in the morning of 24 May, 1683. The nation was in shock. Churchill gave the order: 'Sink the *Bismarck!*'

## The Convergence of the Twain

*Lines on the loss of the Titanic*

I

In a solitude of the sea
Deep from human vanity,
And the Pride of Life that planned her, stilly couches
she.

II

Steel chambers, late the pyres
Of her salamandrine fires,
Cold currents thrid, and turn to rhythmic tidal lyres.

III

Over the mirrors meant
To glass the opulent
The sea-worm crawls – grotesque, slimed, dumb,
indifferent.

IV

Jewels in joy designed
To ravish the sensuous mind
Lie lightless, all their sparkles bleared and black and blind.

V

Dim moon-eyed fishes near
Gaze at the gilded gear
And query: 'What does this vaingloriousness down here?' ...

VI

Well: while was fashioning
This creature of cleaving wing,
The Immanent Will that stirs and urges everything

VII

Prepared a sinister mate
For her – so gaily great –
A Shape of Ice, for the time fat and dissociate.

VIII

And as the smart ship grew
In stature, grace, and hue,
In shadowy silent distance grew the Iceberg too.

IX

Alien they seemed to be:
No mortal eye could see
The intimate welding of their later history,

X

Or sign that they were bent
By paths coincident
On being anon twin halves of one august event,

XI

Till the Spinner of the Years
Said 'Now!' And each one hears,
And consummation comes, and jars two hemispheres.

THOMAS HARDY, 1840–1928

# PLANES, TRAINS AND AUTOMOBILES

Charles Rolls and engineer Henry Royce met on 4 May 1904 and agreed to form a partnership. Charles Rolls sold cars in London, then a prestigious occupation. In July 1906 they produced the 'Silver Ghost' Rolls-Royce. Later on, Rolls met the Wright brothers and became passionate about flight. He was killed when his Wright flyer crashed in 1910.

❖

In 1896 Mrs Bridget Driscoll, aged 44, became Britain's first pedestrian to be killed by a car, despite being hit at approximately 4 mph. She froze in shock on seeing the car and suffered a fatal head injury as she fell. At her inquest, coroner Percy Morrison said he hoped 'such a thing would never happen again'.

❖

In 1897 the first British drink-driving conviction was handed out. Driving a brand-new electric 'Horseless Carriage' taxi with a top speed of 9 mph, George Smith was fined £1 for driving first on the pavement and then into the front of 165 Bond Street in London. Electric taxis would later be withdrawn and the first petrol-engine ones licensed in 1903.

In 1908 the Model T Ford went on sale. It was the first really affordable car and went on to sell 16 million. Henry Ford's production line was a pioneering example of mass production, introducing techniques that would revolutionize manufacturing in the twentieth century.

❖

In 1959 Britain's first motorway, the M1, officially opened. It had no speed limit until one of 70 mph was introduced in 1965. Cars like the E-Type Jaguar were capable of doing almost 150 mph along it until that time.

In 1863 the first section of the London Underground was opened from Paddington to Farringdon Street, the world's first underground railway.

❖

In 1935 Britain's first single-wing fighter plane, the Hawker Hurricane, made her maiden flight. Not quite as fast as the Supermarine Spitfire, Hurricanes could still reach 300 mph and had a smaller turning radius. The plane played a vital role throughout World War II. Douglas Bader flew one in the Battle of Britain.

In 1943 the Dam Busters crews arrived just after midnight at the dams on the river Ruhr in Germany. The bouncing bombs they used were invented for the purpose by Barnes Wallis, who also designed the Wellington Bomber. The Mohne and Eder Dams were breached, but the Sorpe Dam held.

In 1969 Concorde flew for the first time, the result of an Anglo-French project to create a supersonic passenger plane that somehow ended up with the French spelling.

## Odd Days

In England, the first day of April is known as April Fools' Day, in some northern districts as 'April Noddy Day', and in Scotland and the borders it is 'Huntigowk' Day or 'Gowkin' Day. On this cheerful anniversary, any person may be made to look a fool between the hours of midnight and noon.

There are many traditions of practical jokes on this day: the false summons to the door or the telephone, the empty eggshell upside-down in a cup at breakfast, or a sleeve or trouser-leg sewn up.

In Scotland, a 'gowk' is a cuckoo, but also means a fool. Victims might be sent about the town with an unread note which says: 'Hunt the gowk another mile,' and when read, the messenger is sent off again to another house only to be told to go on again. At the stroke of noon all jokes must end. If any attempts are made past midday the intended victim can reply:

April Fools's gone past
You're the biggest fool at last

Or

April Noddy's past and gone
You're the fool and I am none.

## The Daffodils

I wandered lonely as a Cloud
   That floats on high o'er Vales and Hills,
When all at once I saw a crowd,
   A host of golden daffodils;
Beside the lake, beneath the trees,
Fluttering and dancing in the breeze.

Continuous as the stars that shine
   And twinkle on the Milky Way,
They stretched in never-ending line
   Along the margin of a bay:
Ten thousand saw I at a glance,
Tossing their heads in sprightly dance.

The waves beside them danced, but they
  Out-did the sparkling waves in glee:-
A poet could not but be gay
  In such a jocund company:
I gazed – and gazed – but little thought
What wealth the show to me had brought:

For oft when on my couch I lie
  In vacant or in pensive mood,
They flash upon that inward eye
  Which is the bliss of solitude,
And then my heart with pleasure fills,
And dances with the Daffodils.

William Wordsworth, 1770–1850

# FAMOUS REMARKS

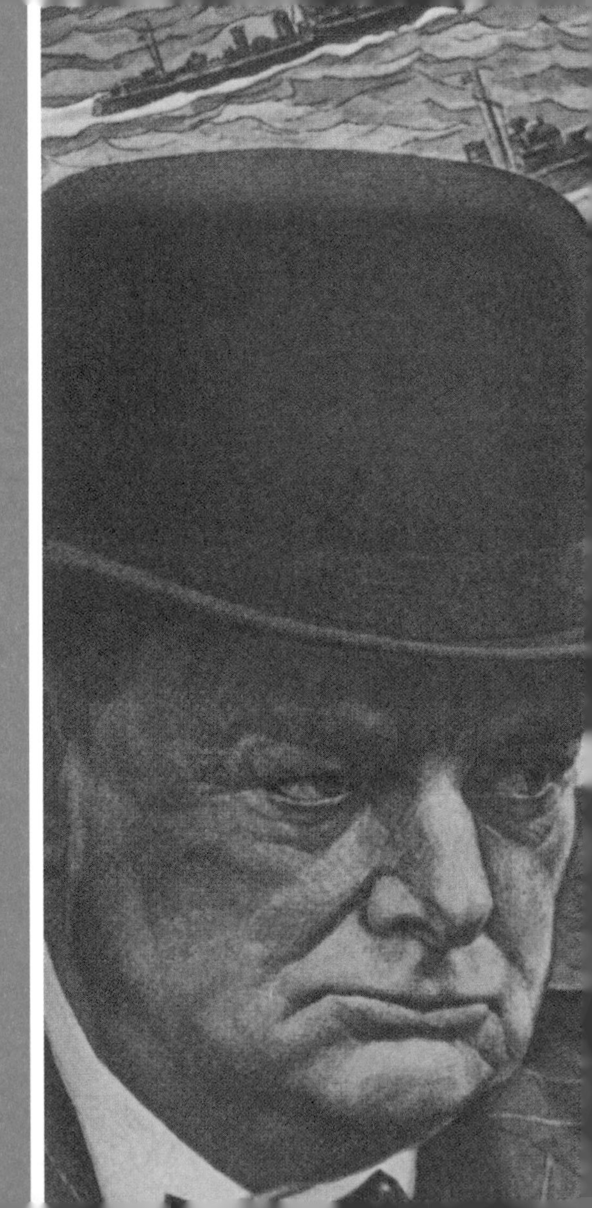

During the second Boer war in South Africa, British forces were besieged by the Dutch Boers for 118 days and lost almost 200 dead. The British commander, Lieutenant General George White, greeted the relief force with the words, 'Thank God we kept the flag flying.'

❖

Captain Lawrence Oates stepped out into a blizzard near the South Pole with the words 'I'm going out, I may be some time.' He knew he had reached such a state of physical collapse that he could only be a hindrance to the others and lessen their chance to survive. His body has never been found.

❖

Neville Chamberlain resigned as head of the government, having failed to preserve 'Peace for our time'.

❖

Churchill became Prime Minister, saying, 'I have nothing to offer but blood, toil, tears and sweat.'

In 480 BC King Leonidas and his Spartans were finally defeated by the Persian King Xerxes at the Pass of Thermopylae. 'Go tell the Spartans, stranger passing by, that here, obedient to their laws, we lie.' As well as the word 'Spartan', they also gave us the word 'laconic', as their region of Greece was known as Laconia. It means a brief, dry wit and comes from an exchange initiated by Philip of Macedon, father of Alexander the Great. He sent the message to the Spartans: 'If I enter Laconia, I will level Sparta to the ground.' They replied with a single word: 'If.'

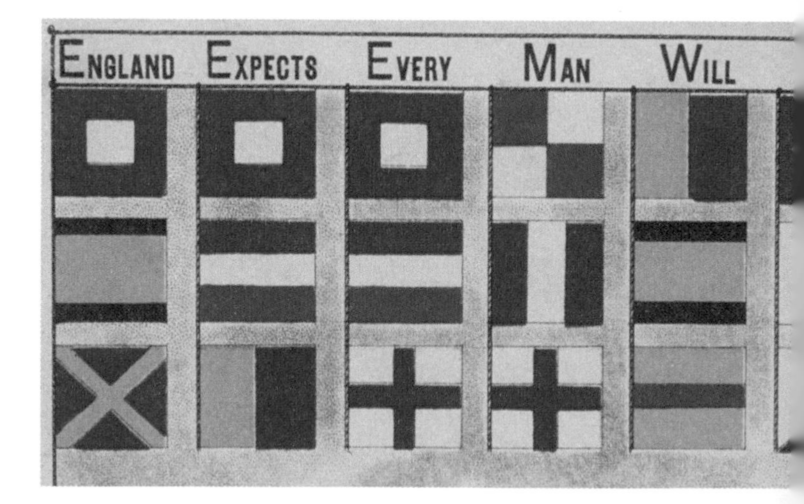

In 1863 Lincoln's Gettysburg Address began: 'Four score and seven years ago, our fathers brought forth on this continent a new nation, conceived in liberty and dedicated to the proposition that all men are created equal.'

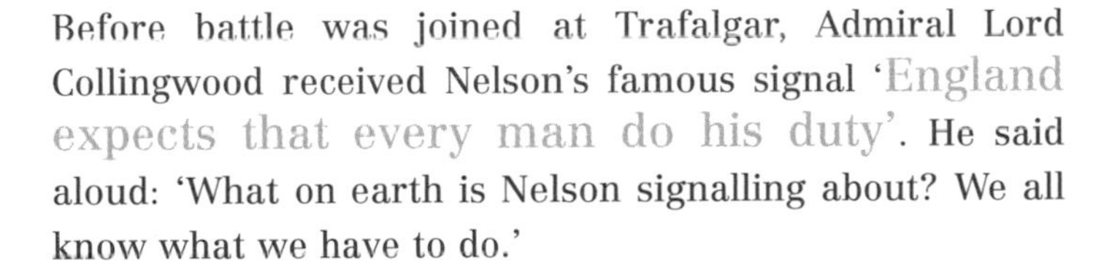

Before battle was joined at Trafalgar, Admiral Lord Collingwood received Nelson's famous signal 'England expects that every man do his duty'. He said aloud: 'What on earth is Nelson signalling about? We all know what we have to do.'

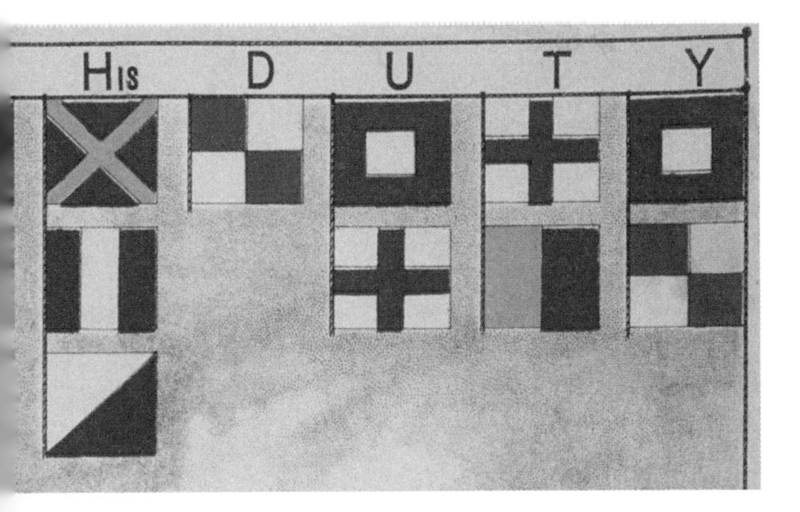

## Kubla Khan
## or
## A Vision in a Dream. A Fragment

In Xanadu did Kubla Khan
A stately pleasure-dome decree:
Where Alph, the sacred river, ran
Through caverns measureless to man
  Down to a sunless sea.
So twice five miles of fertile ground
With walls and towers were girdled round:
And there were gardens bright with sinuous rills,
Where blossomed many an incense-bearing tree;
And here were forests ancient as the hills,
Enfolding sunny spots of greenery.

But oh! that deep romantic chasm which slanted
Down the green hill athwart a cedarn cover!
A savage place! as holy and enchanted
As e'er beneath a waning moon was haunted
By woman wailing for her demon-lover!
And from this chasm, with ceaseless turmoil seething,

As if this earth in fast thick pants were breathing,
A mighty fountain momently was forced:
Amid whose swift half-intermitted burst
Huge fragments vaulted like rebounding hail,
Or chaffy grain beneath the thresher's flail:
   And 'mid these dancing rocks at once and ever
It flung up momently the sacred river.
Five miles meandering with a mazy motion
Through wood and dale the sacred river ran,
Then reached the caverns measureless to man,
And sank in tumult to a lifeless ocean:
And 'mid this tumult Kubla heard from far
Ancestral voices prophesying war!

The shadow of the dome of pleasure
Floated midway on the waves;
Where was heard the mingled measure
From the fountain and the caves.
   It was a miracle of rare device,
   A sunny pleasure-dome with caves of ice!

A damsel with a dulcimer
In a vision once I saw:
It was an Abyssinian maid,
And on her dulcimer she played,
Singing of Mount Abora.
Could I revive within me
Her symphony and song,
To such a deep delight 'twould win me,
That with music loud and long,
I would build that dome in air,
That sunny dome! those caves of ice!
And all who heard should see them there,
And all should cry, Beware! Beware!
His flashing eyes, his floating hair!
Weave a circle round him thrice,
And close your eyes with holy dread,
For he on honey-dew hath fed,
And drunk the milk of Paradise.

SAMUEL TAYLOR COLERIDGE, 1772 - 1834

# GREAT VICTORIES

202 BC saw the Battle of Zama, the final battle of the Second Punic War between Carthage and Rome. After the failure of the original Roman generals, command fell to Publius Cornelius Scipio, better known as 'Scipio Africanus'. His military genius turned the tide of the war. At Zama, Scipio used a mobile formation that could open up to let Hannibal's war elephants trundle straight through. The tactic worked beautifully, neutralizing the threat and one of Hannibal's chief advantages. In the end, it came down to the quality of the fighting men involved, and though the Romans were outnumbered, Scipio had the best Rome could produce. Hannibal was broken and forced to sue for peace, after more than twenty years of war.

In 216 BC came the Battle of Cannae, part of the Second Punic War. The exact date can never be absolutely certain, but the battle was fought in the high summer. It was one of the most crushing defeats ever endured by a Roman army. Hannibal, a Carthaginian general, had a mixed force of many nations. He was outnumbered by professional Roman soldiers and should have been easily routed. Instead, he adopted a cup formation, allowing his own front line to fall back and back until the entire Roman force was trapped and compressed inside the cup. Hannibal's cavalry were superb and held the Roman horse in stalemate while the slaughter continued. The Romans lost between 50,000 and 60,000 men, one of the costliest battles in all history.

At the Battle of Ashdown in AD 871, King Alfred the Great triumphed over the invading Danes.

In 1066, at the Battle of Hastings, William the Conqueror conquered England by beating the exhausted soldiers of Harold after they had marched 200 miles in five days. This was the last invasion of Britain, unless you count William of Orange, who landed with troops, but at the invitation of Parliament.

1340: the Battle of Sluys, the first great battle of the Hundred Years' War against the French. The fleet was personally led by Edward III. Despite roughly equal numbers of ships, the French fleet was annihilated.

❖

1346: the Battle of Crécy, one of the most important battles of the Hundred Years' War. Twelve thousand men under Edward III and his son, the Black Prince, took on 30–40,000 French. The English longbow triumphed. At one point, Edward was told that his 16-year-old son was hard pressed by the enemy. Should reinforcements be sent? He refused, saying his son 'must win his spurs'. The Black Prince fought his way free unaided.

❖

1415: the Battle of Agincourt. This day, 25 October, is also St Crispin's Day. Up to 25,000 French faced 5,000 English. The French knights discovered that 40,000 English longbow arrows fired every minute were a destructive force greater than any the world had ever seen. The practice of sticking two fingers up as an insult comes from this battle. When the French caught an English archer, they cut his bow-fingers off. The gesture came from the English archers, showing the French that they still had their fingers.

1571: the Battle of Lepanto. A spectacular victory against the Moslem Ottoman Empire fleet by Don John of Austria, leading a fleet of Papal forces. It was the last major battle to involve galleys, a form of sea warfare going back many thousands of years. G. K. Chesterton wrote a superb poem about the battle, which begins: 'White founts falling in the courts of the sun ...'

### Oddities

The attempted theft of the crown jewels. One of history's most likeable rogues, Colonel Thomas Blood, had fought against Charles I in the Civil War, and had to flee England when Charles II was restored to the throne. His plan to steal the jewels involved disguising himself as a parson and knocking the Keeper of the Jewels on the head with a mallet. Blood then discovered that the king's sceptre would not fit in his bag. His companion was in the process of sawing it in half when the Keeper of the Jewels came round and summoned help. Astonishingly, King Charles II so enjoyed the man's wit and charm that Blood was not only pardoned, but also given lands in Ireland. Alternatively Blood blackmailed Charles II. We'll never know for certain.

1588: the Spanish Armada set sail from Spain. (Some sources give the date as 29 May.) They reached England in July. They would have set off earlier, but Sir Francis Drake had led a small fleet to Cadiz, destroying up to 60 ships. Drake later referred to this as 'singeing the King of Spain's beard', an action that put back the Spanish preparations for war by a year. Famously, Drake was playing bowls in Plymouth when the Armada was sighted. He insisted on finishing his game before going to his ship. It is true that great storms smashed the Spanish fleet, but they came

after the sea battle, where they were soundly beaten and forced to flee.

The Spanish Armada's attempt to invade England and restore Catholicism had been defeated. The Spanish King, Philip, sent 130 ships to land in Portsmouth, but they were broken by better seamanship and gunnery off the coast of Dorset and the Isle of Wight. Over the next few weeks, the remnants of the Armada were scattered by fireships and then pursued all the way north to Scotland before the chase was called off.

1657: the Battle of Santa Cruz, the greatest victory over the Spanish since the Armada in 1588. Sixteen Spanish ships were destroyed by an English fleet commanded by Admiral Blake.

❖

1746: the Battle of Culloden, the final clash between the Jacobites and Hanoverians in the second Jacobite Rebellion of 1745. The Jacobites supported the right of Charles Stewart, better known as Bonny Prince Charlie, to the throne of England and Scotland. They were defeated and George II remained in power.

❖

1757: the Battle of Plassey, part of the Seven Years' War. Robert Clive, later known as 'Clive of India', was outnumbered many times, fighting the forces of the Nawab of Bengal and French artillerymen. Despite the odds, Clive pulled off an incredible victory, helping to secure the British position in India and denying the French their claim.

1759: the Battle of Minden in the Seven Years' War. A vastly outnumbered column of British infantry routed eleven squadrons of French cavalry, an incredible feat of arms. It is still celebrated by the regiments who had men in that mixed column. As the British column advanced, they passed through a garden and took roses to wear in their hats. On 1 August each year, 'Minden Roses' are worn by serving and retired men of the Suffolk Regiment, the Royal Hampshires, the Lancashire Fusiliers, the Royal Welsh Fusiliers, the King's Own Yorkshire Light Infantry and the King's Own Scottish Borderers.

❖

In 1763 the Treaty of Paris was signed, ending the Seven Years' War – by far the most successful war in British history, which is saying something. It brought India and Canada into the fold, denying those territories to France. The French nearly won it all back with Napoleon, of course, but 'nearly' is quite important in these matters.

1798: the Battle of the Nile. One of the French ships destroyed was Napoleon's flagship, *L'Orient*. Nelson collected some of the timbers and had them made into his coffin. Famously, he had to be pickled first in alcohol to keep him fresh for the trip home after Trafalgar. Legend has it that a good deal of the liquor had been drunk. Nelson's final tomb in St Paul's sits close to Wellington's and Admiral Collingwood's, Nelson's friend who commanded the Trafalgar fleet after Nelson's death.

1794: 'The Glorious First of June'. The Channel fleet under Lord Howe gained a famous victory over a French fleet under Villaret de Joyeuse. Six French ships were captured and one sunk. After that, the French Admiral wasn't particularly 'joyeuse' at all. In Britain the day is still commemorated under the same name.

1801: the Battle of Copenhagen. Nelson's victory is one of four actions commemorated on his column.

1809: the Battle of Oporto took place during the Peninsular War in Portugal. An Anglo–Portuguese force under Wellington defeated the army of Marshal Soult, capturing 1,500 and killing 600 for a loss of only 120 men. As a result, Napoleon's armies were forced to retreat from Portugal. On the night of 12 May Wellington sat in the French headquarters and ate the meal that had been prepared for Soult.

### Oddities

In the thirteenth century, the King of France presented Henry III with three lions for his menagerie kept at the Tower of London – a gift which became part of the royal coat of arms. The image of three lions can still be seen on English sporting jerseys today. The King's collection of exotic animals was a subject for mockery amongst the courtiers. On the first day of April, the King invited his court to witness the lions washing and bathing in the Tower moat. When they arrived that morning, there were no lions to be seen.

1812: the Battle of Salamanca. Wellington had intended to pull back from Spain to Portugal after six weeks of tactical sparring with French forces under Marshal Marmont. When he saw a gap open on Marmont's left flank,

Wellington shouted, 'By God, that will do!' and ordered an attack. The victory was a crucial step in the Napoleonic wars. A French general commented of Wellington: 'He manoeuvred like Frederick the Great, in oblique order.'

In 1815 the Battle of Waterloo took place: the final destruction of Napoleon's second attempt at power after escaping from the island of Elba. Arthur Wellesley, Duke of Wellington, was in command of 93,000 Allied forces: British, Hanoverians, Dutch, Belgians, Brunswickers and Nassauers. He was ably supported by 117,000 Prussians under Marshal Gebhard von Blucher.

❖

On 22 January 1879 the battles of both Isandlwana and Rorke's Drift were fought. Eleven Victoria Crosses were awarded.

❖

1942 the Battle of Midway in the Pacific ended. It began on 4 June with Japanese air raids on the US military base on Midway Island, a 1,000 miles north of Hawaii. The American response involved the Pacific fleet. They sank or damaged ten Japanese destroyers and four aircraft carriers, losing none of their own ships. Admiral Chester Nimitz of the Pacific fleet said of the battle, 'Pearl Harbor has now been partially avenged.'

In 1945 Japan surrendered at last. VJ day (Victory over Japan) is celebrated on 15 August.

◆

VE day, 8 May 1945: Victory in Europe, as German forces finally surrendered after six years of the bloodiest war in history. Allied countries including Britain, Canada, Australia, New Zealand, America and Russia lost more than 60 million men, women and children in the conflict.

In 1982 the Battle of Goose Green took place during the Falklands War. Despite being outnumbered two to one, the British forces were successful in routing the Argentinians after fierce hand-to-hand fighting. Lieutenant Colonel H. Jones was posthumously awarded the Victoria Cross. In addition, twenty other military decorations were awarded for gallant service and heroism.

### Oddities

Remembrance Day, 11 November, commemorates those Britons who have died in wars, giving their lives for the peace and freedom of those they left behind. Services are held around the country on Remembrance Sunday, the closest Sunday to the eleventh. A two-minute silence is held nationally at 11 a.m. on Remembrance Sunday and also on 11 November if it falls on another day. In the weeks before Remembrance Sunday, red poppies are sold everywhere by the British Legion, a tradition going back to 1921. The poppies are made in one place by ex-servicemen and women, where 70 per cent of the workers are disabled or suffer from chronic illness. The money raised goes to help the widows and orphans of those soldiers as well as the survivors.

# FAVOURITE AUTHORS

Sir John Betjemen, poet laureate from 1972. His best known works include 'A Subaltern's Love Song' and 'Slough'.

❖

Rudyard Kipling, the first British author to be awarded the then new Nobel Prize for Literature in 1907. A superb writer of prose and poetry, Kipling is best known for his novel Jungle Book and the poem 'If'.

❖

The poet, artist, visionary and genius William Blake, born in London in 1787. He is perhaps most famous for writing 'Jerusalem', which begins, 'And did those feet in ancient times ...' and 'The Tyger', which is about a tiger.

❖

William Shakespeare. In 1582 he married Anne Hathaway by special licence. He was eighteen. She was twenty-six and pregnant. They had three children together. He went on to become the most famous playwright of any age. His best works include *Macbeth*, *Henry V*, *Romeo and Juliet*, *King Lear*, *Hamlet* – too many to list. He is also the author of hundreds of sonnets. Perhaps the best known of them begins: 'Shall I compare thee to a summer's day?'

Wilfred Owen, perhaps the best-known poet of World War I. Owen had been sent home to a war hospital in Edinburgh, suffering from shell-shock. There he met fellow poet Siegfried Sassoon who was recuperating from a head wound. Sassoon told Owen he would 'stab him in the leg' if he tried to return to France, but Owen felt it was his duty. Only seven days before peace was declared, he was shot and killed as he was crossing a canal. His most famous poem is 'Dulce et Decorum Est'.

Aldous Huxley, born in 1894. His most famous novel is *Brave New World*. Another book, *The Doors of Perception*, details the author's experience with mescaline, a hallucinogenic drug. The title comes from a line of Blake's poetry: 'If the doors of perception were cleansed, everything would appear to man as it is: infinite.' The title was later used by Jim Morrison to name his group 'The Doors'.

P. G. Wodehouse (Pelham Grenville), born in 1881. The creator of Jeeves and Bertie Wooster, Psmith and Ukridge, he is the author of more than ninety books and one of the great comic writers of the twentieth century.

H. G. Wells, born in Kent, wrote novels which have become classics of science fiction, often showing extraordinary insight into the future. His most famous works include *The Time Machine*, *The Invisible Man*, *War of the Worlds*, *The Shape of Things to Come* and *The Island of Dr Moreau*.

❖

Enid Blyton, born in London in 1887. She became the most famous children's author in history, with instantly recognizable creations such as *The Famous Five*, *The Secret Seven*, *The Magic Faraway Tree* and the Noddy stories. All of these are still read today. In all, she wrote around 800 books.

❖

William Golding, who also won the Nobel Prize for Literature. By far his best-known novel is *Lord of the Flies*, a book about boys turning savage on a desert island.

❖

George Orwell (real name Eric Blair), one of the greatest writers and thinkers of the twentieth century. His most famous works are *1984* and *Animal Farm*, though he was also a superb essayist and proponent of clear English.

Charles Dickens, one of the great names in literature. His most famous works include *Oliver Twist*, *David Copperfield*, *A Tale of Two Cities*, *Great Expectations*, *Nicholas Nickleby* and *A Christmas Carol*. All of these have been filmed and some have even become musicals.

❖

Kenneth Grahame, author of *The Wind in the Willows* which was published in 1908. It became a classic, introducing the world to Rat, Mole and the wonderful Mr Toad of Toad Hall.

❖

John Anthony Miller, better known as the author Peter Pook. His books are hilarious.

❖

Mary Wollstonecraft Godwin, better known by her married name of Mary Shelley. She is most famous for her novel *Frankenstein*. A vegetarian herself, she also made the monster of the book one, which dampens down the horror somewhat. The thought of him clumping through the night after a nut cutlet doesn't create quite the terror you might expect.

Jerome K. Jerome, the author of *Three Men in a Boat*, a strong contender for the funniest book ever written.

❖

Dr Samuel Johnson, born in 1709. He was a celebrated essayist, poet, wit and critic, much of his life recorded by his biographer James Boswell. Johnson is best known for *A Dictionary of the English Language*, which he wrote over nine years. One of the better-known definitions from it is: 'Lexicographer: A writer of dictionaries, a harmless drudge'.

❖

J. R. R. Tolkien, whose *The Fellowship of the Ring*, the opening book in The Lord of the Rings trilogy, was first published in the United Kingdom in 1954. The trilogy went on to be extraordinarily successful.

## Jerusalem

And did those feet in ancient time
Walk upon England's mountains green?
And was the holy Lamb of God
On England's pleasant pastures seen?

And did the Countenance Divine
Shine forth upon our clouded hills?
And was Jerusalem builded here
Among these dark satanic mills?

Bring me my bow of burning gold!
Bring me my arrows of desire!
Bring me my spear! O clouds, unfold!
Bring me my chariot of fire!

I will not cease from mental fight,
Nor shall my sword sleep in my hand,
Till we have built Jerusalem
In England's green and pleasant land.

William Blake, 1757–1827

# DANGER POINTS

1962, the Cuban Missile Crisis developed. President Kennedy announced the discovery of Soviet missile sites in Cuba. He demanded publicly that they be removed, and for six days the world tottered on the brink of nuclear war. The Soviet leader, Nikita Kruschev, blinked first and agreed to remove the missiles.

❖

1942, the second battle of El Alamein took place in Egypt, where Axis powers were forced to retreat. After three vicious years of war, this was a crucial victory and boost to morale for the Allies. Famously, Churchill described it as 'Not the beginning of the end, but, perhaps, the end of the beginning.'

❖

1943, Italy declared war on Germany, having seen which way the war was going.

❖

1938, Prime Minister Neville Chamberlain returned from a meeting with Adolf Hiltler in Munich in which Hitler stated his desire not to go to war with Britain. Chamberlain waved the agreement and declared it to represent 'peace in our time'. World War II broke out less than a year later.

1759, James Wolfe defeated the French at Quebec in Canada in the Seven Years' War, changing the history of a continent. Both he and the French commander died in the battle. Wolfe's navigator was James Cook, who would go on to discover Australia, the 'Terra Australis' that was the stuff of legend right up to him running a ship into it.

❖

1620, the Pilgrim Fathers set sail for the Americas in the *Mayflower*. A Puritanical religious group, they had suffered in England and were looking for somewhere they could practise their faith. They had set out the day before in two ships, but the *Speedwell* leaked and had to dock at Plymouth in Devon. It was from Plymouth that the *Mayflower* finally left, landing at last on the east coast of North America. Once there, the Pilgrims sought out a suitable place to begin a colony and ended up in a location they also named Plymouth, in Massachusetts. They were not the first English people to make the trip, nor were they the first successful colony, but they were by far the best known and have become part of American history, usually involving something to do with turkeys.

AD 467, Flavius Romulus Augustus was deposed by the Germanic chieftain Odoacer. Romulus Augustus was the last of the Western Roman emperors, so this date is sometimes given as the end of the Roman Empire, though the Eastern Roman Empire around Constantinople survived for centuries after this date.

❖

On 1 May 1707 the Act of Union came into effect, joining England, Wales and Scotland. The first article of the Act described the Union flag as a combination of the cross of St Andrew and the cross of St George. The final design also incorporated the cross of St Patrick of Ireland. British ships fly the flag on the jackstaff, which is why it is often called the 'Union Jack'. On land, it is properly called the 'Union Flag'.

❖

1979, Margaret Thatcher became the first woman to be Prime Minister. She served three consecutive terms.

1948, the State of Israel was declared, sanctioned by the United Nations. The following day, the British mandate in Palestine expired and the armies of Egypt, Syria, Jordan, Iraq and Lebanon all attacked at the same time. Israel fought them all and forced each country to accept an armistice in 1949. Hostilities continued throughout the twentieth century, with outbreaks such as the 1956 Suez Crisis, where Israel fought with Britain and France against Egypt, and the 'Six Day War' in 1967, when Israel was again attacked by Egypt, Jordan, Iraq and Syria. Despite almost constant conflict with Arab nations, Israel has survived for the last sixty years. The region remains in crisis into the twenty-first century.

❖

1879, the Zulu king, Cetewayo kaMpande, was eventually captured by the British after the Battle of Ulundi earlier in the month. His capture marked the end of the Zulu wars, which included events like Isandlwana and Rorke's Drift. Cetewayo was sent into exile and died five years later. Zulu tribal lands become part of the Union of South Africa, making Cetewayo the last independent Zulu king.

# ILLUSTRATIONS

# DANGEROUS THINGS I HAVE LEARNT

***From dinosaurs and insects to the solar system.***

The perfect pocket book of the wonders of the world for every boy from eighty.

***From girls to battles, from anthems to pirates and naval codes.***

The perfect pocket book of things to know for every boy from eight to eighty.

***Build a treehouse, become a conker champion, master knots.***

The perfect pocket book of things to do for every boy from eight to eighty.

***The Original and the Best.***

The perfect book for every boy
from eight to eighty.

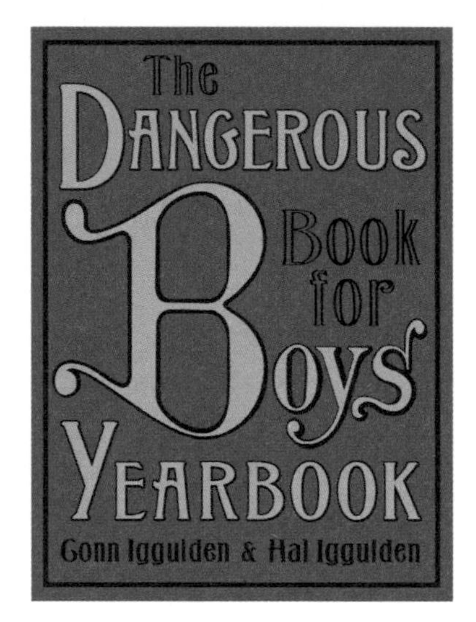


***An event for every day, a story for every month.***

The perfect yearbook for every boy from eight to eighty.